Contents

CHAPTER ONE ....

CHAPTER TWO 9

CHAPTER THREE 18

CHAPTER FOUR 24

CHAPTER FIVE 34

CHAPTER SIX 43

CHAPTER SEVEN 51

CHAPTER EIGHT 55

CHAPTER NINE 62

CHAPTER TEN 69

CHAPTER ELEVEN 74

CHAPTER TWELVE 81

CHAPTER THIRTEEN 89

CHAPTER FOURTEEN 98

CHAPTER FIFTEEN 109

CHAPTER SIXTEEN 117

CHAPTER SEVENTEEN 128

CHAPTER EIGHTEEN 137

CHAPTER NINETEEN 144

CHAPTER TWENTY 155

CHAPTER TWENTY ONE 164

CHAPTER TWENTY TWO 170

Chapter one

Siobhan groaned wearily as the alarm blared into life, how could radio DJs be so bloody cheery at 5.45am! Next to her, her husband grunted, *it's alright for him*, she thought, *he hasn't got to be up for another hour.* She gingerly stepped out of bed, damn it, she'd forgotten to change the heating, it meant it wouldn't come on for another hour and the house was bloody freezing.

Leaving her husband snoring she grabbed her dressing gown and made her way downstairs. Tea, that was her first priority, with a cup of tea inside her she could start to contemplate the long day ahead. *Where was she meant to be today? That was it, Stoke, a horrible case of child abuse, a client who ticked every stereotypical paedophile box going, and a Judge who didn't conform to the new ideal of "user friendly"* -old school was the best way to describe him.

Whilst the kettle boiled Siobhan ran through what needed doing before she could leave the house, the kids' school lunches needed making, the washing had to be put on, and Ben needed some money sending in for a school trip.

She wasn't hungry but she forced a piece of toast down, knowing it would be hours before she got chance to eat anything else. The dog eyed her suspiciously from his basket, too warm and cosy to actually get out of his basket and come and say hello, but at the same time wanting to be fed.

As her tea cooled she threw a suit on, it had seen better times but money was tight at the moment and a new suit wasn't a priority, as long as it didn't have dried cereal or toothpaste on the lapel it would do, besides she could always wrap her gown around the worst stains.

Danny started to stir in bed, "You alright, love?" "Yeah, just heading off. Don't forget Emily's got netball tonight so you need to pick her up at 4.30pm, and make sure Ben takes the money for his school trip in." "'K". She knew he was only half listening but she would message him later, she filed another job to her mental list.

Siobhan grabbed her suitcase, made a final check of her papers and then headed for the car. It was frozen over so she began silently cursing as she tried to scrape the frost from the windscreen. She managed to create a small window of clear glass, and got in the car, hoping that the rest of the screen would clear before she hit the motorway. God, she hated the cold, bring on summer, summer meant not having to leave home in the darkness, it meant some much needed time off, it meant a change to routine drudgery that her life had become. It wasn't that she was resentful, she knew that on the face of it she was more fortunate than most, decent job, nice house, hefty mortgage, husband, two kids. Just at 44 she was, well, bored. Life consisted of alarm clock, work, home, dinner, prep work for the next day. Weekends were a blur of tennis, music lessons, school parties; she had nothing for herself. A treat was to order a Chinese on a Friday night and try not to fall asleep in front of Have I got news for you.

The radio was blaring in the car and her favourite Killers song came on, shaking her mind awake a little. *Get a grip*, she thought, *stop being so sodding needy,* there were people out there who would kill to have her life, take today's case for example, her client was 58 and accused of sexually abusing his step daughter when she was a child. The stepdaughter was now in her 30s but her life was a wreck, she had turned to drink, her own children were in and out of Social Services care and she lived in a grotty one bedroom flat in a rough area of Stoke. Now that was a hard life.

The M6 was its usual Monday morning car park and the two hour drive passed interminably slowly, eventually Siobhan parked up and made her way down the urine soaked stairwell.

The security staff took pride in their jobsworth reputation and despite the fact Siobhan had been visiting that court for the last 22 years of her professional life they still insisted on her emptying her handbag, removing her water bottle to have a sip of water – proving she hadn't brought acid to court on a whim. The alarm beeped as she walked through the security arch, so she then had to be checked over with a wand.

"Got anything metal on you"

"Just my hip" joked Siobhan. Her "joke" received a dead eyed stare. "Empty your pockets."

"I already have done, I haven't got anything in them."

"Well you'll have to go through again"

For fuck's sake she thought, she went through her pockets and found a penny lurking in the bottom of her trouser pocket. Typical, last year a man had managed to bring a knife to court and stab his partner in the court room, but she had been stopped because she had a rogue penny on her person.

Eventually she got through and made her way to the robing room. She was gasping for a cup of coffee but the court cafes had long since been shut down and the vending machines were obviously out of order. She dumped her bag on the table and logged on to the court computer to see who her opponent was. The name flashed up on screen, Gerry Berkshire. Siobhan groaned, Berkshire was 80 if he was a day, he should have retired long ago but he was one of those barristers who would die with his wig on. He was curmudgeonly, patronising and deeply unpleasant to be against, he was also a bit "hands on", Siobhan vowed one day she would pluck up the courage to knee him where it hurt but she knew she never would, she liked a quiet life and didn't go looking for trouble.

The robing room was quiet, she had made it in before 9am, before the madness descended. She had one final last look through her notes and then went into the public area to meet her client.

9.15am, no sign, no sign of Berkshire either, he was probably in the CPS room, trying to persuade the 20 something year old caseworker to go out for lunch with him, he really did have the hide of a rhinoceros!

Finally, her client arrived, Siobhan grimaced as he came through security, why did he have to wear that shabby grey mac. With his few remaining hairs greased over his scalp, a two day growth of stubble, and stained corduroy trousers he had just made her job infinitely more difficult. She drew her shoulders back, took a deep breath, and plastered a fake smile on her face.

"Mr Holland, how nice to see you again"

"Eh up duck, how are you doing?

"Very well, thank you. Shall we find a conference room?"

Siobhan looked along the corridor, trying to find a conference room that didn't smell of sweat and despair. Eventually she found one, it had 3 chairs, which was a bonus, and some of the paint was yet to peel away from the wall.

"Come on in, Mr Holland," she ushered him into a seat, "How are you feeling today?"

"Well that's a stupid bloody question isn't it" he snapped, "I'm on trial for sexually abusing that slag, looking at prison for something I ent done, and you're sitting here asking me how I'm feeling!"

Siobhan bit her tongue, "Yes, of course, I appreciate you must be under great strain, are you physically fine, and ready for the trial?"

"Aye, I just want it over with now"

"Of course, I understand. Well, as I've explained previously the trial will last about 4 days. We will hear the Prosecution's case opening this morning. You won't agree with what they are saying but they are telling the jury what their case is. After that the jury will watch the video interview of your stepdaughter"

"Lying cow"

"I know that's how you feel, but if you say anything like that in court the jury won't take kindly to you. Try and keep a hold of your emotions, we can chat at every break and you can vent to me then in private. Once the video has played I will then cross examine Tracy, she'll be in court but behind a screen so that only the Judge and jury can see her"

"What's wrong with her looking me in the eye as she spins these lies about me?"

"I've explained already Mr Holland, complainants in sexual cases are automatically entitled to special measures, in this case Tracy would like to be in the court room but she'd prefer not to have to look at you. The Judge will tell the jury that they mustn't hold it against you in any way, it's perfectly normal in these types of cases."

Bernard Holland grunted, "Still don't understand why she gets special treatment."

Siobhan spent the next 45 minutes patiently going through court procedure, checking her points for cross examination, and also explaining the worst case scenario if he were to be found guilty. She hated that bit, it always felt as if you were telling the client that you had no faith in their case and that this was what they could expect to happen. Sometimes she felt like Jim Bowen "And this is what you could have won – 7 years at one of her Majesty's finest establishments." She checked herself and came back to Mr Holland, "So, if you could go and wait on the concourse now, the usher will call us on when the court is ready for us."

She watched as he lumbered out of the conference room. Right, she couldn't put it off any longer, she'd better go and find Gerry. She made her way down the stairs and headed for the CPS room.

"Morning Syreeta, I'm defending in Holland, any sign of Gerry yet?"

"Hiya Siobhan, yeah he was around earlier, I think he's gone to speak to the witnesses, he'll be back out shortly I reckon."

"Ok, could you tell him I'll be in the robing room?"

"Course I can, see you in a bit, I'm covering court 2 so I'll be up there."

"Thanks, see you shortly"

Siobhan went back to the robing room, she only had to wait a couple of minutes before Gerry appeared, red faced, and out of breath.

"Morning Gerry, have you been running?"

"My dear woman, if CPS insist on putting the witness waiting room at the far end of the building this is the result! Now, is your man going to see sense and put his hands up or do I have to prosecute this pile of nonsense."

"Gerry, its sex, it's a Stoke jury, you know and I know that he won't plead, we'll just have to go through the motions."

At that moment Siobhan noticed a young woman standing just behind Gerry, she thought the woman looked familiar but couldn't quite place her. Gerry noticed her looking,

"Siobhan, meet Miss Niamh O'Brien, chambers pupil. Her supervisor is way so she's with me for the week"

Niamh looked up shyly, "Hi" was all she said.

She was tall, with short dark hair and dark brown eyes, she was so thin that Siobhan thought one gust of wind might knock her over. Her face was elfin like, delicate cheekbones and a mouth that was on the cusp of smiling.

"Nice to meet you Niamh. Tell me, do you spend your life spelling your name to people too?" Niamh smiled in a knowing way, "I guess so, back home its Ok but here its " Ni – am" or "Neem."

Her accent was beautiful, a real soft Northern Irish. Siobhan smiled back, "Sy -oh – ban is my usual, some days I feel like sticking a sign on my forehead "Its pronounced Shiv-orn!"

Niamh smiled again, and Siobhan found herself staring at her for a second too long. She cleared her throat.

"So, erm how's pupillage, I don't think we've actually met before"

"Ah, its going Ok, I've met some lovely people, I'm finding it quite tiring, guess I'm not used to all the travelling, but I'm really enjoying it. I think I saw you in chambers when I was having my induction."

"You should have said hello, it's important for pupils to get to know new members of chambers"

"Ah well you looked busy, I wouldn't have wanted to interrupt. I did want to say hello though, I read about one of your cases in the Law reports and wanted to talk about it"

"My one and only success in the Court of Appeal you mean!" Siobhan was flattered, she had been to the Court of Appeal a few times on standard appeals against sentence but she'd only had genuinely interesting appeal against conviction on a point of law and it had been picked up by a number of the formal law reports, she couldn't believe that not only did Niamh know of the case but that she also knew it was Siobhan who had defended in it.

"When I got offered a place in pupillage I did some research on the members and your name came up for that case, I remembered reading about it in law school and couldn't wait to actually meet you in person"

"Well, that's very impressive research, Brownie points for you!"

"I'd love to hear about it one day, if you get chance?"

"Absolutely, maybe when the jury go out at some point. Well you should be in for an interesting case this week, familial sex abuse, welcome to the glamourous life of the Bar!"

They stood there for a moment in silence before Gerry spoke. "Well my witnesses are here so if I've got to do this damn case let's get on with it shall we."

Ever the gentlemen, thought Siobhan. "Ok, let's go up to court and see where we are in the list"

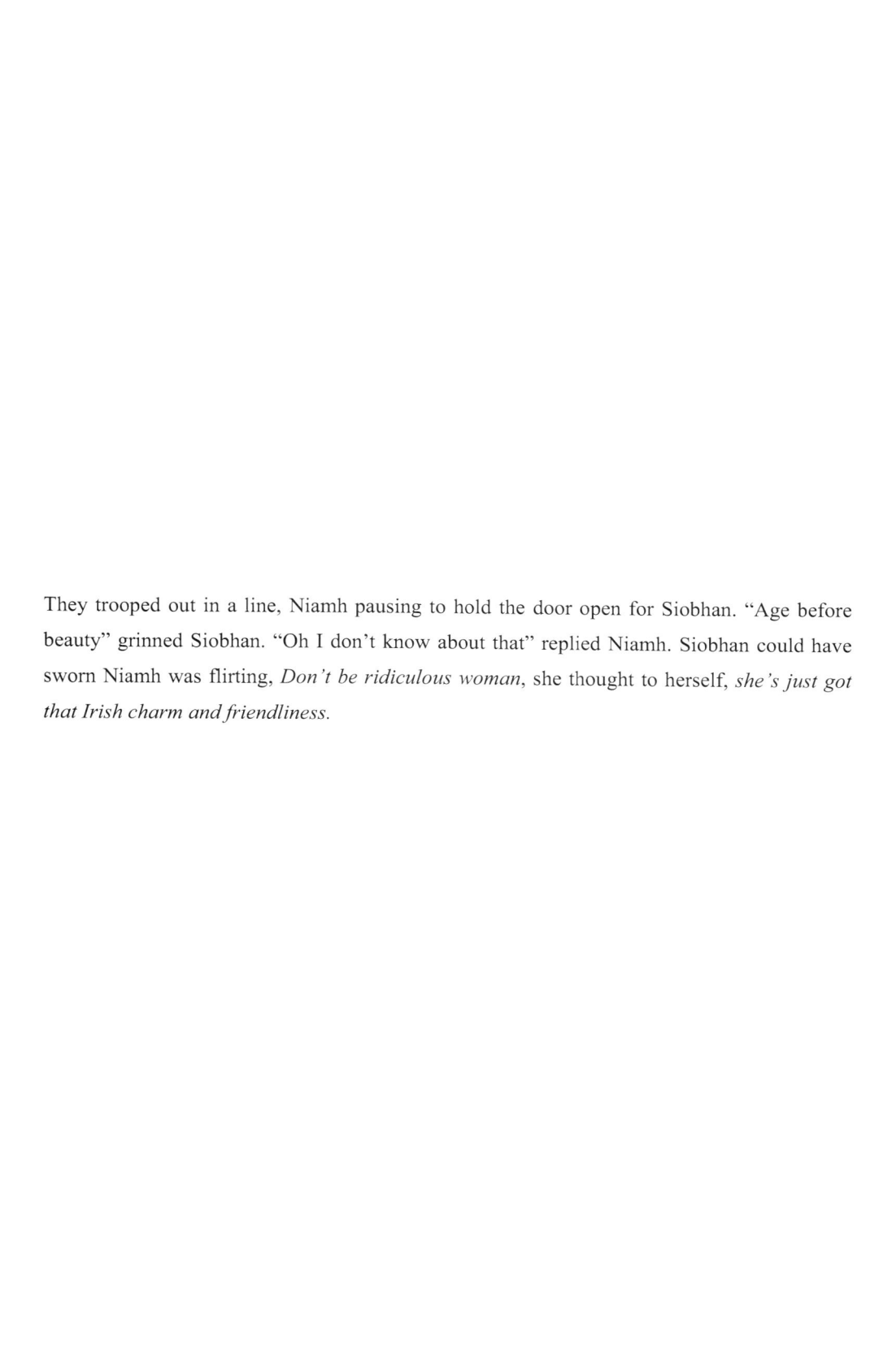

They trooped out in a line, Niamh pausing to hold the door open for Siobhan. "Age before beauty" grinned Siobhan. "Oh I don't know about that" replied Niamh. Siobhan could have sworn Niamh was flirting, *Don't be ridiculous woman*, she thought to herself, *she's just got that Irish charm and friendliness.*

Chapter two

"Court rise". His Honour Judge Cavendish came into court. "A trial are we?" All of the advocates nodded. Siobhan could have sworn she actually heard him sigh "Well, better get a jury panel then, anything I need to worry about before the trial starts?" Before Siobhan could open her mouth to speak he continued, "Fine, let's get on with it then."

Trials involving historical sexual abuse are pretty formulaic, the Prosecutor tells the jury what the complainant in the case says has happened to her, for it is usually a her. The jury are handed an indictment containing the counts that the defendant faces, which bodily appendage he has placed in which hole – there is a surprising array of combinations- then the video of the crying victim is played.

Siobhan's mind drifted, the video lasted an hour and a half, with the Police officer firstly asking Tracy to tell her everything that had happened, and then going back over it again in painstaking detail. It was the patronising manner that the Police sometimes asked questions that really grated with Siobhan, "So you say he put his willy in your mouth, can you tell me what you mean by willy?" This was a 35 year old woman who'd had three kids, of course she knew what a bloody willy was! The questions went on, Siobhan had a transcript of the video in front of her but she had read it so many times in preparing the case that she really didn't have to follow it as the video played out to the jury. She thought about lunch, bugger, she had forgotten to make a sandwich, that would mean she'd have to go into Hanley and pick up something during her lunch break, mind you she needed some new tights too as the ones she was wearing had just started to go a bit saggy, she could pop to Marks and Sparks and get them there when she grabbed her lunch.

"Miss Flaherty" Although she was married she was still referred to in court by the name she had been called by. It helped her to separate her life, Mrs Smith at home, Miss Flaherty at court.

Siobhan looked up. "Well, Miss Flaherty?"

"Sorry, Your Honour, I didn't quite hear that"

"I said how long will you be in cross examination!"

Siobhan hadn't even noticed that the video had stopped playing. All of the jurors were looking at her expectantly and she was fairly sure Berkshire was smirking into his counsel's notepad.

"Erm, about 40 minutes Your Honour"

"Well, we'll take a short break and carry on, I'd like you to finish this witness before lunch"

"Of course"

They rose, Siobhan turned her phone on to see she had 12 Whatsapp notifications. Most of them were from Danny

"What time does Emily finish netball?"

"When is Ben's school trip?"

"What time will you be in tonight?"

She sighed, began to answer them and then her client asked if he could have a word. Before she knew it the break was over and she was back in court. She had lost count of the number of times she had cross examined this type of offence. There were only so many ways you could put the case, basically that the complainant, for some unknown motive, was lying, and out to get her poor innocent client. Unsurprisingly she made no progress with Tracy whatsoever and all she succeeded in doing was annoying the jury and making Tracy cry.

Another solid morning's work, she thought to herself bitterly. She went through the motions with her client, explaining why she hadn't "Tried to destroy the bitch" and that she had questions for other witnesses which would make some inroads.

She was just about to escape when Berkshire called her over "Siobhan, could you show Niamh where the M&S is, I want a sandwich but it's too bloody cold for me to go out. There's a dear"

Naturally he didn't offer to pay for his own sandwich. *Grumpy bugger, he knew the rules,* thought Siobhan, *Pupils don't pay for anything, their Pupil Supervisors get them lunch.*

"Come on Niamh", she said, "Let me show you the delights of Hanley – and grab your scarf, its grim Oop North!"

They started up the hill towards the town centre, past the old snooker hall where on a Friday you could still get fish, chips and a pint for a fiver. Across the road, navigating from pawn shop to bookies.

"So, Niamh, how's pupillage going?"

"Good, so far, I think. I mean, it's still early days yet but I'm enjoying it."

"How come you've chosen to work here rather than back home?"

"Well I don't know if you know the system over in Northern Ireland? But basically, we don't have chambers like youse do. Sorry, you. We all work from the Bar library which means you have to try and build up your own practice from scratch, there aren't returns from other Barristers to get you going. That's fine if your Mammy or Daddy has plenty of money, or you have lots of lawyer contacts, but I don't have any of those, so I came over here for Bar school and then was lucky enough to get pupillage, so here I am."

"Here you are indeed", Siobhan smiled to herself, she knew how hard it was to forge a career at the Bar, especially as a woman, especially doing crime, it was nice to see some genuine enthusiasm for a change. She suddenly felt very old, and very tired, it had been a while since she had felt that passionate about anything.

"Who is your normal Supervisor"

"Oh, it's John Evans, he's been grand, we've done a fair few trials in Wolverhampton, and Stafford, a week in Worcester- I'm certainly getting to see the Midlands!"

"Where are you living?"

"My partner and I have got a place in the Jewellery Quarter, its handy for getting into chambers and to the train station."

"Do you not drive?"

"No, the pupillage award only goes so far, and besides, most courts are by a train station so it's not too bad."

"Bet you cursed when you got to Stoke this morning then didn't you?"

"Oh, aye, a mile and a half walk with my suitcase wasn't exactly what I had planned!"

"How are you getting back?"

"I dunno, guess I'll walk the same, least I know the way now"

"I could give you a lift if you want?" Siobhan wasn't sure why she had just offered that, she barely knew the girl, the station wasn't particularly convenient to get to, and all she usually wanted to do when she had finished in court was get home, yet here she was blurting it out.

"That would be grand, if you're sure you don't mind?"

"Of course not" – the most British words tripped off her lips before she even thought about it.

They were almost at Marks and Spencer's.

"Go and get a sandwich for yourself and Gerry, and I'll meet you at the tills, I just need to pick up something." Siobhan stopped short of saying she wanted to buy some tight, why? Was she embarrassed? It was so stupid, she didn't want to talk about mundanities in front of this perky young pupil – what was wrong with her?

Minutes later and lunch was purchased, Siobhan looked guiltily at her sandwich, chocolate, crisps, fizzy drink, meanwhile Niamh had gone for sushi and fruit – maybe that's why she's so thin and I'm kidding myself that this size 12 suit jacket still fits.

They walked back to court, "So, have you followed everything that's been happening today?"

"I think so," Niamh replied "Except I wasn't sure why you didn't ask the victim"

"The complainant" Siobhan interrupted

"Sorry?"

"At the moment she is a complainant, victim implies that the defendant is guilty, which, given he is having a trial, means he is innocent until proven guilty."

"Oh" said Niamh, chastened.

"I'm not telling you off, just it's important to get the language right when you are dealing with cases like this."

"I get it, sorry. Anyway, so why didn't you ask the complainant about what she'd told her friend about the alleged abuse"

They spent the rest of the walk back to court discussing the finer points of cross examination, the tactics of dealing with differing versions of complaint and how unused material was your best friend in cases like this.

In the robing room Gerry was complaining about how long Niamh had taken to bring his lunch back. Siobhan bit her tongue.

The afternoon passed slowly as Siobhan went through the motions with the role call of friends to whom Tracy had complained. She knew that she could be better than this, knew there were probably killer points but if there were they were eluding her now. She just wanted the day to be over and to be away from the institutional smell of court.

By 5pm court had risen and she had been able to rid herself of her client. She put her coat on, it was dark outside and was just starting to drizzle, oh joy, the M6 would be hell.

Gerry struggled to fasten his coat over his ever expanding frame, "I'm off, dinner tonight with an old chum from college. Niamh, make sure you are back here for 9am tomorrow morning, and I expect you to have edited the defendant's interviews and emailed me the draft agreed facts"

"Yes, Mr Berkshire"

"Gerry!" He snapped, "You're a member of the Bar now, girl, first names only!"

"Sorry, yes, sorry, Gerry"

Siobhan looked on, she felt sorry for this youngster, learning the idiosyncrasies of the Bar was never easy, and when your teacher was Gerry Berkshire, no wonder the poor kid looked crestfallen.

"Come on, Niamh" she said, "Hop in the car and I'll drop you at the station"

They walked to the car park in silence. The car was freezing and it took Siobhan a few minutes to warm it up and for the condensation to disappear. They sat there awkwardly whilst the blowers did their work.

"Anything nice planned for tonight?" She asked eventually.

Niamh smiled ruefully, "I guess that wild night out clubbing is on hold"

Siobhan looked at her shocked.

"Sure, I'm only joking! Monday night for me is usually a heady mix of University Challenge and Only Connect, but I guess tonight Gemma is going to have to watch it by herself, seeing as I have interview editing to get done"

"Gemma, is she your housemate?"

"Erm, no, my partner"

"Oh". Siobhan tried to play it cool, and failed miserably. She racked her brains to try and think of something to say that wouldn't come across as deeply unfashionable or over the top "down with the kids." "Where did you two meet?" was her lame attempt.

"Bar school, we were both at Nottingham together and then we found out we had both joined Gray's Inn, you know what dining sessions are like, couple of bottles of red, two glasses of port later and we were inseparable"

Siobhan remembered those days well, boozy nights and raging hangovers, she smiled at the memory.

"Are you married?"

"Yes, 14 years now, Danny and I met at a club. Believe it or not I was once able to strut my stuff on the dance floors of the Midlands." Siobhan paused, she was trying to remember the last time she and Danny had actually been out together, just the two of them – did a quiz night at the kids' school last month count? Probably not.

"Have you got kids?"

"Yes, two, the regular nuclear family. Emily is 12 and Ben is 9. They're good kids" She didn't know why she had to justify like that, who was going to say their own kids were horrible?!

"Gemma and I have talked about kids, but not just yet. Is your husband a barrister too?"

"No, thank goodness, I spend all day talking to lawyers, the last thing I want to do is come home and spend my evening talking law too! He's an electrician." She struggled to think of anything to add, it wasn't that his job was boring, it was just, well what more could you say about being an electrician. They lapsed into silence once more.

Siobhan turned the car into the waiting area across from the station, "There you go. What time train are you getting in the morning, I could swing by and pick you up from here if you want?"

"That would be great, yes please. It gets in at 8.52 I think, thank you so much, you're a life saver!"

"Hardly. Anyway, you have a nice evening and I'll see you in the morning"

"Thanks, G'night"

Siobhan watched as Niamh disappeared into the station, then she put the car in gear and set off for home.

She pulled onto the drive just after 6.30pm, it was sleeting again as she got out of the car and put her key in the lock.

"Hi love"

Danny was sprawled on the sofa, the TV blaring, Hollyoaks on. God, she hated that programme. "Good day?"

"Yeah" was the grunted response.

"Busy?" She ventured.

"Bit, yeah"

She gave up and went to seek out the children. Ben was in his room, headphones on, his Xbox showing some violent car jacking game, Emily was in her room, on her phone, involved in at least 3 separate Snapchat conversations. They at least acknowledged her before turning back to their respective devices and their own little world.

Siobhan couldn't wait to take off her suit, and the itchy, cheap tights. She looked in her wardrobe, contemplated putting on some nice jeans but settled for her leggings and a baggy jumper – plus ca change.

"What's for dinner love?"

Danny looked at her, confused. "Me and the kids had the leftover curry from the weekend, I think we finished it"

Great, knackered, starving and the arsehole hadn't even done any dinner. She opened the fridge and looked at it expectantly, as if a meal would somehow materialise from between the cheese and half opened packet of bacon. In the end she gave up and opened the freezer, she grabbed one of the ready meals for one that lurked at the back and flung it in the microwave.

Four minutes later and she was eating what was purportedly a lasagne, but would give cardboard a run for its money in terms of blandness. Another four minutes and it was gone. Another gourmet meal in the Smith household.

She put her plate in the dishwasher and opened up her laptop at the kitchen table, she dreamed of a purpose built study, somewhere she could retreat to, glass of red on the leather topped desk, classical music playing softly in the background, her own haven. Instead she cleared some of the family detritus away and began to plough through the dozens of emails that had arrived whilst she was in court.

By 9pm she'd had enough, she went into the lounge, Danny hadn't moved, an ITV drama was playing out on the TV.

"Anything on?"

"Not really"

"Anything different happen on site today?" She didn't know why she was even bothering to try.

"Nah, Gaz called in sick, think he overdid it a bit at the weekend, daft sod."

That was the end of the conversation. She sat there for a few minutes longer before realising she hadn't told Ben to get into bed. She went up to see him, like father like son, he hadn't moved and the xbox was still flashing away.

"Ben have you done your homework?"

"Didn't have any"

"Ok, well can you turn that off now and get ready for bed please?"

"Just 10 more minutes?"

"No, now, it's already past your bedtime"

"Moo—oo-mm"

"No Ben, now, please, before lose my temper."

Ben huffed as he turned the console off. "Night Mom"

"Night darling, make sure you read for a bit"

"'K"

She stuck her head around Emily's door, "Bed by 10 please"

"Alright, night"

Siobhan didn't bother going downstairs to see Danny, he was still engrossed in the tv and she was shattered. She pulled her pyjamas on and crawled into bed, her eyes were swimming with details of the emails she'd been through, and her stomach felt heavy as the barely digested lasagne lay on it. She closed her eyes and let the sleep come.

That night she dreamt of Niamh.

Chapter three

The sleet had turned to freezing rain as she pulled up on the car park outside Stoke station. She couldn't help but smile to herself when she saw Niamh running across the road, trying to dodge the taxis and the raindrops.

"Morning"

"Morning, thanks again for the lift, I'd have been soaked by the time I got to court!"

"No problem, I was passing anyway"

For the next three days it became her ritual. Niamh's train would pull in just before 9 and Siobhan would be waiting for her. She looked forward to their chats as Niamh relaxed in her company.

"So when we got to Borneo we were in this filthy hostel, there was no electric, the water only ran for two hours in the morning and then two hours at night, but it was totally worth it just to get to see the orangutans at the sanctuary"

Siobhan dreamed of travelling somewhere like Borneo, even the name of it sounded exotic. She and Danny went to Tenerife every year with the kids, they had first gone when they had been together for about a year and Danny proclaimed that he didn't need anything else. "You've got the sun, the hotel, pool, beach and cheap beer – what more do you want from a holiday?" In theory, yes it ticked all the boxes people looked for on holiday and she knew there were many people for whom a foreign holiday every year was a luxury they could only dream of, but like the study she just wanted something more. Being a barrister people expected you to live a glamorous jet set lifestyle, but somehow it hadn't worked out like that. Criminal legal aid had been slashed, the kids always seemed to need expensive new trainers, or a laptop for school, and somehow they were getting by but trips to places like Borneo, or Peru were just not on their radar, even if she could persuade Danny to leave his beloved Tenerife.

"Of course if you want wild animals then you have to go to on safari, there is nothing so majestic as seeing lions feasting on a zebra as the sun rises over the bushland."

"How have you had chance to travel so much?"

"Well my Daddy went into property just before the Irish tiger really started to roar, and he sold at the peak of the market, meant we had a pretty nice life growing up, mind you, he spent it well enough too, money had all gone by the time I was due to go to university."

Siobhan sat silently for a short time, her mind on an exotic Safari trip. The grey concrete of Stoke Crown court soon brought her back to mind numbing reality.

The trial was due to finish today, the Judge had summed up yesterday and the jury were being sent out at 10.30am to consider their verdict, it meant she just had to sit and wait for the inevitable. Her client had been terrible giving evidence, vindictive, rude, arrogant – everything a jury hated, so now it was only a matter of time.

Berkshire arrived at court at 10.20am, "Nothing for me to do now" he declared loudly, "I nailed the bugger in cross examination and the jury were nodding like dogs at my speech. Your boy will be starting a fair old stretch tonight I'd have thought."

Siobhan raised an eyebrow in acknowledgement, ok her client had been crap but he didn't need to rub it in. She sat in the robing room feeling tired and fed up.

They were tannoyed into court, the ushers were sworn and the jury were sent out. This was the worst part, analysing what had happened in the trial, wondering where she could have taken a better point, thinking about her closing speech. Endless self reflection and laceration.

She was jolted out of her thoughts by the appearance of Niamh beside her

"Thought you might want this", Niamh was holding a coffee from the newly repaired vending machine, "You looked miles away"

"Yeah, just replaying the speech in my head"

"Do you always do that?"

"What? Go over my cases? Yeah, I can't help myself"

"Gees, you'll go to an early grave"

"It's important, you've got to look at every case and see where you went wrong and what you could do better. It's the only way to improve"

"Life's too short. If you spend every second analysing what you did wrong you never live in the moment"

Spoken like a 20 something thought Siobhan. Someone who hasn't got to worry about where the next brief is coming from to make sure the mortgage is paid.

Niamh took a seat next to her. "Sorry if that sounded rude, I do want to learn an all, but if you spend your life just worrying then you never enjoy what's right before your eyes" She looked straight at Siobhan. Siobhan felt herself going slightly pink. Thankfully the tannoy in the robing room burst into life "All parties in the case of Holland to court 2 please"

Siobhan found her client in the waiting area and explained that the jury had now reached a verdict, she reminded him to try and not show any emotion, but she didn't hold out much hope of him following that advice.

Forty minutes later, the guilty verdicts had been returned, her client was now downstairs in the cells starting a lengthy prison sentence. She felt exhausted by it all, the grubbiness of the cases, the emotion of endless victims, the self righteousness of her clients. She rubbed her eyes and began to pack up her robes and papers, knowing she would have a long list of cases to deal with tomorrow. She realised she ought to go into chambers too as she hadn't been in all week and she dreaded to think what was in her pigeon hole.

Berkshire was leaving at the same time as her "There, there old girl, I can't help it if the jury like my debonair approach. Oh, are you going into chambers? Couldn't drop these in for me could you?" He waved some discs of evidence around.

"Yeah, I'm going in, anything else need dropping in?"

"Actually, could you take Niamh with you, I'm out of court tomorrow and I think her regular supervisor is back so she needs to speak to the clerks."

"No problem, come on Niamh, if we leave now we'll miss the worst of the traffic"

Niamh followed behind her as they returned to the car park. Twenty minutes later and they were driving through Staffordshire, the sun doing its best to lighten the gloom of the November day.

"There's some lovely countryside around here isn't there?" Niamh said, surprised.

"Yes, it always surprises me just how green England is"

"I still feel like I'm getting to know the place, I've basically been to Nottingham and London, now Birmingham, but I haven't really been out much, you know"

"We're just coming up towards Lichfield way, have you ever seen the Cathedral there?"

"No, never heard of it to be honest with you"

Siobhan checked her watch, 3.45pm. She knew she still had to get to chambers, check her pigeon hole, pick up any work for tomorrow, and then make it back in time for Ben to get to Cubs, yet still she heard herself saying "Come on, let's stop off and I'll show you what you're missing"

Lichfield on a cold Thursday in November is not over run with tourists and Siobhan found a spot near the Cathedral easily enough. When the children were younger they used to come here for the Bower, a May Day celebration with fair rides and a parade. When was the last time they had had a family day out like that?

"This is Dr Johnson's tea shop, it does the most wonderful home baked scones, come on, I'll treat you"

The smell of coffee lifted her spirits and they found a table nestled in the corner, but which still afforded a magnificent view of the Cathedral.

"I don't do this sort of thing very often"

"What, take a pupil for coffee?"

"No, I don't mean that" flustered Siobhan, "I just meant, take a bit of time for myself, without rushing between work and the kids"

"Maybe you took on board what I said earlier, live a bit more for the moment"

Siobhan didn't reply, she felt confused, and excited. She felt as if she was doing something wrong, but all it was just a coffee for Heaven's sake. So why did she feel guilty, why was she enjoying spending time with this young woman. She felt Niamh staring at her. "This was lovely, thanks Siobhan."

"Oh it was just coffee"

"I know, but you've been so lovely to me this week, I was dreading it when I first met Gerry, but you've just been so welcoming, and I feel like I've learned a lot too. It's a shame I have to go back to my regular Supervisor on Monday"

"Who are you going to be with tomorrow"

"Don't know yet, the clerks are going to tell me once they've sorted the lists out"

"I've got a bunch of cases in Stafford if you want to tag along? I can't promise anything as exciting as another dirty perv like Holland, but you'll get to see a variety of types of hearing"

"That would be amazing, thank you"

"I still have to go into chambers though so we'd better get going."

"Thank you again" Niamh put her hand on Siobhan's. Siobhan flinched, shocked, both at Niamh and also her own reaction, she pulled her hand away. Niamh just smiled at her.

"Erm, come on, we need to go" She put her coat on hurriedly and left the café, not looking back to see if Niamh was following her. Her heart was pounding and she felt embarrassed, but also, if she was being honest with herself, excited. She turned round and saw Niamh a couple of feet behind her. She didn't know what to say, perhaps she was reading into the situation something that just wasn't there.

"Gosh its cold out now isn't it" – great, resort to talking about the weather when you're in an awkward situation.

"Aye, it is. Look, if you drop me at chambers I'll see if anyone else is free tomorrow"

"No, its fine, I said you could come with me, and I meant it". Siobhan took a deep breath and steadied herself. "Please, it would be nice."

Niamh smiled at her again, "Alright, thanks"

The journey into chambers took another 40 minutes, Siobhan desperately racked her brain for conversation, anything to break the awkward silence that had enveloped them.

"What attracted you to criminal law Niamh?"

"I guess the frustrated actress in me, isn't that the case for most criminal barristers? I love being the centre of attention, when you're cross examining or making a speech the jury is your audience and all eyes are on you, I love that buzz!"

"For me it was the chance to live vicariously, my life is just so quiet and ordinary, and yet the cases you come across and the stories you deal with, it's just exciting isn't it. Well it used to be, it doesn't feel like that now, I think I've seen enough misery to last me a lifetime, problem is I'm not qualified to do anything else!"

"Have you thought about the Bench, or Silk"

"No chance, my career is what can only be described as average, nope, this is me for the next 20 years. God, that's depressing isn't it!"

"It doesn't have to be, you don't have to accept that this is it you know"

"Ah, the optimism of youth!"

"There's no need to patronise me" Niamh sounded hurt.

"Sorry, guess I've become a bit more cynical than I realised"

"Have you got time to talk about the Court of Appeal case now?"

"Absolutely, and I'll try not to be as cynical"

The rest of the journey was taken up with Siobhan detailing her experience before Lord Justice Thomas and how she had almost been late for that fateful hearing. Niamh was laughing along as Siobhan regaled her with her battles against the tube and taxis that morning, the panic she had been in when she finally got to court, then the hearing itself. The drive flew by and Siobhan found herself wishing the journey would last a little longer.

"So, I guess I'll see you tomorrow. If you could be at court for 9.30am that would be helpful, the court is right next to the station so you should be able to find it ok."

"Ok, thanks and I'll see you tomorrow"

Siobhan mechanically checked her pigeon hole, spoke to her clerks and did all the little jobs that needed covering. It was now gone 6.30pm and she was going to be late for Ben and Cubs if she didn't hurry up.

She ran to her car, there on the windscreen was a note "Sorry if I made you uncomfortable today, it's just nice to admire a strong woman at work. N x"

She smiled to herself, and let out a breath she didn't even know she had been holding. Then it was home to the madness.

Chapter four

A lie in until 6.45am, the luxury! Ben needed his PE kit re packing, he appeared to have been mud wrestling at school last night and Danny hadn't put it in the wash, she'd found it shortly before she was due to go to bed and had sworn under breath when she saw the state of it.

She tried to engage with Emily, who had her buried in her phone. "Do you want to go anywhere this weekend, maybe shopping together?"
Emily looked at her as if she had two heads.

"I'm meeting my friends in town"

"Ok, just a thought. So, what have you got at school today?"

"Same as always"

She didn't know why she bothered. "Ok, well have a lovely day and I'll see you at home later"

She picked her suitcase and called up the stairs, "Dan I'm off, bye Ben, have a good day"

Ben at least replied with a muffled "Bye Mom", she heard nothing from Danny.

Friday traffic was always so much easier and she made it to court in good time. Seven cases today, four of which were sentences, then a PTPH and a couple of mentions, with any luck she'd be done by lunchtime.

"Morning Miss" It was Jules, Security Guard at Stafford, he'd been there since she'd been a pupil and he was one of the loveliest guards she came across. "Who you in front of today then?"

"Goose"

"Ah, well you haven't heard then, he's called in sick, his cases are being split between Donaldson and Griffiths"

"Oh bollocks"

Jules grinned, "Knew you'd be pleased!"

It meant Siobhan was now split between two different courts, trying to juggle both clients and judges, the lists would be longer, and Griffiths was notoriously slow, rising after every mitigation to run and find another Judge to help him with the sentence. The prospect of an early finish seemed very distant now.

"Don't suppose any of my clients have arrived yet?"

"Who you got, here's the ones who've signed in with us"

One had arrived, not bad, she'd get changed and try and get a start with Probation and speaking to her clients. "Oh, I've got a pupil with me today, Niamh O'Brien, can you point her in the direction of the robing room when she gets here?"

"Tall, Irish, dark hair?"

"Jules, how do you know these things, yes!"

"She was here early, didn't recognise her so asked who she was, she looked fresh out the box so I guessed she might be a newbie, she's in the robing room now"

Siobhan punched in the code for the robing room and opened the door to find Niamh at the central table, two fresh lattes from Costa sitting before her.

"Morning, thought you might need this to get you going"

Siobhan smiled gratefully, "Thanks, having just been told about my Judge this is exactly what I need"

"I heard, something about splitting the lists?"

"Yeah, so basically I am now before two different Judges with my cases listed at the same time, it's called being cross courted and it means I have to be in two place at the same time, neither Judge will understand, and I will succeed in pissing off my clients when they turn up to get sentenced before a Judge who I have put in a bad mood. Great Friday eh!"

"Well if I can help?"

"Thanks, the coffee is a good start. Come on, let's go and see if any of the punters are here"

They walked upstairs and found Sue, the usher for court 3.

"Sue, hi, I was meant to be in front of Goose today but now I'm in your court – listing have split my cases though – I'll be in court 4 too if you need me"

"Hello Miss Flaherty, righto, thanks for letting me know. You know what His Nibs is like though, I'll juggle what I can but if you keep him waiting too long he'll be spitting feathers"

"I know, but what I am supposed to do? I'll try not to keep him waiting but I've got sentences in front of Griffiths too"

"You'd be able to do most of your cases in front of Donaldson whilst Griffiths rises won't you?" chuckled Sue.

Siobhan grinned, the staff were renowned for their sense of humour but they also knew what their Judges were like and Sue clearly had some sympathy for the situation Siobhan found herself in.

The morning was a disaster, her first case was called on before Griffith at 1115, and at 1225pm Griffiths was only just finishing passing sentence. Siobhan dashed out of court to Donaldson's court. Ominously there was no one in there except for Sue

"Bollocks! Has he finished his list?"

"No, but everyone is cross courted so he's stomped out in a huff"

"Sorry! I'm ready on my cases with him now"

"Ok, but you'll need your oppo, let me know when you've got a full house of both counsel and clients"

Siobhan dashed to the robing room, frantically trying to find anyone who was ready in her cases, she spotted Jane Edmonds in the corner, "Jane, are you good to go on the Ali case"

"Absolutely, is Donaldson free"

"Yep, but we've got to get on now otherwise we'll be here all bloody day"

Donaldson stormed into court at 12.35pm. "Miss Flaherty I have been waiting 40 minutes for you"

"Yes, I'm sorry Your Honour, I hadn't intended to be cross courted but your Learned brother Judge becoming ill I'm afraid my cases were split between yourself and His Honour Judge Griffiths"

"So you thought you'd choose Griffiths over me did you?"

There was no right answer to that, Siobhan just shrugged and apologised again.

By 1pm when the court broke Siobhan had completed just two of her cases, bloody brilliant, 5 still to go on a Friday afternoon.

"Come on, let's get some fresh air"

Siobhan and Niamh walked into Stafford together, choice were limited now that the Marks and Spencers was closed so Siobhan opted for Boots – can't beat a meal deal bargain.

"Ok, so you know what cases I've got left, tell me how you would have gone about preparing the mitigation for them"

"Well I guess I would start with the sentencing guidelines for each offence, then look at the mitigating and aggravating circumstances, and then look at the personal mitigation."

"Excellent, that's just how you should approach it. Also, make sure that you tell the Judge at the start of your mitigation what it is you will be asking for, so if you are trying to get a suspended sentence, tell the Judge that so he knows where your mitigation is going"

"Gotcha"

Siobhan really enjoyed this side of the job, teaching, training, watching someone at the beginning of their legal career learning how not to make mistakes.

They spent the rest of the lunch break chatting through Siobhan's remaining cases and talking about the best way to approach them.

It was a long afternoon and it was gone 4.30pm by the time Siobhan finished her last case.

"I need a bloody gin!"

"Well, we could go for one?"

"No, I should get home, Emily has got netball practise tonight and I said I'd pick her up"

"What time does it finish?"

"5"

"Well, its 4.36 now, you're not going to get back to Four Oaks now for 5 are you?"

"FUCK!" Siobhan was tired, tired of always being late, never being there when she said she would, tired of being shouted at for things that weren't her fault.

"Look, if you've missed it already you may as well stay for one drink"

"Fuck it, you're right. Come on, there's a nice little pub in the town centre, mind I can only have one"

She texted Danny to say she'd be late "Just going for drink with friend"

She could have said which friend, but she didn't. Normally she would, yet something held her back and she didn't know what.

The Swan was starting to get busy, the Friday workers just finishing for the week and piling into the pub to meet their friends. Siobhan found a quiet booth in the corner. "Drink?"

"Gin sounds good to me"

Siobhan went to the bar and ordered two gin and tonics, she carried them back carefully to the booth.

"To the end of a bloody long week"

"Cheers to that"

They both sipped their drinks and sat there in a comfortable silence for a few minutes, just letting the stress of the week wash over them.

"Have you enjoyed your week Niamh?"

"Very much so, I know today was stressful for you but honestly I find it quite useful to just watch and understand how a day like that unfolds."

"I'm glad one of us enjoyed it!"

"I didn't mean I enjoyed watching you get a bollocking, I meant, it showed me what the reality of life is like, and I don't think I'd really seen that before."

"They're not always that bad, but yeah, sadly they happen too frequently for my liking. Come on then, what's been the most useful thing you've learned this week?"

Niamh paused, "I'd say, how to look calm under pressure. You're unflappable and I really admire that"

Siobhan went pink "I guess it's just years of practise. Anyway, cheers, to Friday"

"To Friday"

Siobhan's phone buzzed "When u back?" It was Danny, she looked at her watch. "Soon, just finishing drink"

She had no desire to rush and finish her drink, the weekend held a round of netball, music lessons, and play dates – plus her work for the following week, but she knew she should get a move on.

"Niamh this has been really nice, thanks, but I'm sorry, I've really got to get going."

"Yeah, of course, totally, thanks again for everything this week"

"I'll see you around chambers maybe?"

"Yes, I don't know which courts I'm in over the next few weeks but I'll be sure to look out for you"

"Are you coming to the crime group party next Friday?" This was the annual criminal group piss up, ostensibly it was a marketing exercise, a thank you to all the solicitors who had sent work into chambers over the last few months, in reality everyone and the office cat turned up and would do their best to drink the bar dry.

"I don't think pupils are invited"

"Oh well, that's a shame. I'll see you around though"

"Um, would it be ok if I took your number, just you know, when I get on my feet it would be handy to have some people to call on"

"Er, yeah, no, that's fine. Here, give me your phone and I'll type it in." Siobhan added her number, she then called herself from Niamh's phone "And now I've got yours too, should anything come up"

"Great, well, have a lovely weekend and I'll see you soon. Bye Siobhan."

"Bye Niamh"

Siobhan picked her bag, wrapped her scarf tightly around her and disappeared into the gloomy night. She felt that tingle in her stomach again and tried to ignore it as she walked to her car.

feeling, she couldn't think of the last time her family had asked her how her cases had gone. She felt a little thrill every time a new message popped up, was it just the attention she was enjoying or did it go deeper than that? She was flattered, she knew that much, this young, attentive, bright, attractive young woman wanted to chat with her and Siobhan hadn't realised just how much she had been missing that kind of attention. It didn't mean anything more than that, she told herself, just someone being kind. And yet, yet, that thrill, it felt wrong, but exciting, she knew she wouldn't be telling Danny about the fact she had been chatting with this woman – surely if it was all so innocent she wouldn't be thinking like this, or feeling a warmth in her groin that she hadn't felt for a long time.

"When's dinner?"

Siobhan jumped, she hadn't heard Danny come in.

"Er, when Emily gets back, I was going to order pizza. That ok?"

"Yeah, I might just grab something before then, I'm starving"

"OK, love. I'd better go and collect Ben soon anyway. I'll drop Emily a message and see if she's going to be home soon."

Saturday evening was spent before the TV, the family ate in silence, X Factor blaring out of the TV, the pizza being devoured.

"How about a family game of something? "Siobhan asked brightly

"Yeah!" at least Ben was enthusiastic. Emily rolled her eyes and Danny just looked confused.

"God Mom you are so embarrassing, what are we, like 7?"

"I just thought, you know, we don't spend that much time together anymore, now we're all here why not take the chance"

"But X Factors on"

Siobhan bit her tongue, "Just an idea, that was all"

No one replied.

"Think I'll go up for a bath"

She left them sitting in silence and went upstairs to the bathroom. She began to run the bath, then decided she might as well have a glass of wine too, so she raided the cupboard and found a merlot lurking at the back, hiding behind the cereal.

The bath was glorious, and she sank underneath the water, letting it roll over her eyes, enjoying the throbbing sound in her ears. Her mind played over the week, the coffee with Niamh, the gin, the exchange of messages. Her fingers slipped down towards her clitoris and she began to idly rub herself. Images of Niamh flashed into her mind and she pictured kissing her, imagining what those soft lips felt like, how it would to slip her tongue inside her. She came in a matter of seconds and sat up in the bath, panting. She felt ashamed and embarrassed, but also more sexually turned on than she had done in years. She searched for the wine and took a long drink, then rested her head against the bath. Fantasy, that's all it was, something a bit different to her daily life, it wasn't going anywhere, just a silly little crush that allowed her to escape the humdrum monotony that her life had become.

She towelled dry and went downstairs, no one had moved from the sofa. "I'm going to read in bed for a bit"

Danny vaguely looked in her direction and nodded, the kids didn't turn their eyes from the TV. Siobhan made sure she had the wine and went upstairs to bed.

Chapter five

Monday, Stoke, sex. Siobhan felt thoroughly unmotivated, but she forced herself through the week. The M6 was hell, the client vile, and the weather grim. By the time Friday came around she was exhausted.

Her phone buzzed with an email at 9am, it was a round robin from the clerks

"DON'T FORGET, CHRISTMAS PARTY TONIGHT, ALL BAR ONE 6PM ONWARDS"

Why did they have to send messages in bloody capitals? It was like they were shouting at her. She hadn't forgotten about the party but she really wasn't in the mood. Trouble was these things were a three line whip by the clerks, they expected you to turn up, schmooze the solicitors and CPS, make polite conversation and encourage the work to come into chambers. It was the last thing she wanted to do after a long week, but she knew she had to go.

She messaged Danny "Don't forget, got chambers party tonight. Will be home late"

She had told him this morning but she was fairly confident he hadn't been listening.

The jury came back in her trial just after lunch, not guilty, so after the usual thanks and handshakes she was able to escape fairly swiftly. She decided against going home, and chose instead to drive to chambers and leave her car in the car park there – she would pick it up at some point over the weekend.

Steve, her clerk, was on the phone when she got in. She waited whilst he finished

"Hiya Steve, any news on next week's work yet?"

"Hi Miss, nah, still sorting the diary. You around for this bash tonight?"

"Yeah, thought I'd come in early and do a bit of work before wandering over."

"Sound, I think we're on for a decent turn out, CPS are sending about 25 over, chance for you to have a word with some of them and maybe try and get a few more briefs"

Siobhan sighed, she hated making small talk with lawyers she barely knew, on the off chance they might send her some work, but she knew what was expected of her. It was always made easier with a couple of gin and tonics inside her.

She had a quick wander through chambers, to see if there were many people she knew in, Sarah and Parmjit were chatting in the common room. She decided to join them.

"Hey stranger" said Parmjit, "Long time no see"

"Yeah, I've been stuck in the wilderness of Stoke for bloody ages, I've managed to cultivate a practice up there – completely unintentionally!"

Parmjit grinned, she knew how grim Stoke could be and felt some sympathy for her colleague. "Have you come in for the chambers bash?"

"Yeah, clerks emailed me to make sure so thought I'd better show willing"

"Ah, it won't be that bad, few G&Ts inside you and you'll be rocking up the dance floor."

Siobhan smiled, it had been a while since she had rocked any dance floor, she wasn't a natural exhibitionist and avoided dance floors at all costs.

"Come on" said Sarah, "Let's go for a cheeky one before it gets started"

Siobhan didn't take much persuading and they found themselves in The Old Contemptibles, gins in hand. It had a reputation as a bit of an old man's boozer but Siobhan loved the period detail, it still had all the old tiles, along with heavy red drapes at every window, it just had an atmosphere that a lot of the newer pubs didn't have.

"So, what you been up to, any goss?" asked Sarah, she was perennially cheerful, known to enjoy a drink and she had been looking forward to the party for ages.

"Nothing new, same old"

"Wow, exciting stuff"

"You wait till you're mid 40s, with two kids, then tell me how exciting your life is"

"God, no thanks, I do not want kids! I prefer footloose and fancy free. Ooh, talking of which I've heard Michael, that gorgeous solicitor from Browns and Co is coming tonight"

"Oh come on Sarah, he's young enough to be your son" Parmjit laughed at her friend incredulously.

"What? A girl can dream can't she? You're only as old as the man you feel, and I reckon I feel about 25"

"You are joking aren't you, he won't have eyes for you, especially not with some of our new lot coming?"

"How dare you, who can possibly rival me for glamour", Sarah tossed her hair jokingly, a glint in her eye as she challenged Parmjit.

"Have you seen our new pupil? Legs to her bloody armpits, gorgeous, and she knows it"

Siobhan said nothing, but her ears pricked up

"Who's that then?"

"Oh, whatshername, she's Irish, John Evan's pupil"

"Niamh" said Siobhan quietly

"Yeah, that's her, every time she walks in the clerks' room the boys stop what they're doing and look at her with big puppy dog eyes"

"They're pathetic aren't they" Sarah rolled her eyes "A pretty face and they don't care what's between the ears."

"I don't think they've got much chance with her" said Parmjit knowingly, "I don't think our boys do it for, if you know what I mean?"

"Ooh do tell!"

"Well I've heard she bats for the other side!"

"No way, that pretty and gay! Michael will be gutted"

"What does it matter if she's gay" interjected Siobhan

"It doesn't" Sarah said, puzzled, "It's just funny watching the clerks panting like dogs and I bet they don't realise they don't stand a chance!"

They sat in silence for a moment.

"Are you ok?" Sarah asked finally

"Yeah, just been a long few weeks that's all, sorry, didn't mean to snap at you"

"That's alright, I think you need another drink"

They got another round in and Siobhan could feel the gin taking its effect, she felt more relaxed than she had done in a while.

"I didn't think pupils were allowed to our Christmas do?"

"Oh, the clerks think it might be a good marketing strategy, Niamh has to go round with the champagne, topping up the drinks, that way she can introduce herself to a load of solicitors"

"Are we back in the 70s" scoffed Parmjit, "They wouldn't do that with the male pupils!"

"I'll speak to Steve, I can see that getting her to meet new solicitors is a good idea, but I'm not sure treating her as a glorified waitress is the right way to go about it"

"Look, its nearly 6, do you want to head over, might as well make the most of the free booze before CPS turn up en masse and nab it all"

The three of them walked up the road to All Bar One, it was starting to fill up already and they had to fight to get a glass of champagne from one of the waiters.

Siobhan found herself chatting to various solicitors and members of the Bar she hadn't seen in a while, the music was blaring and, despite herself, she was having a good time.

"Champagne madam"

Siobhan was just about to wave the waitress away when she turned to see Niamh standing there holding the bottle out.

"Hi" she said shyly.

"Hi yourself"

"You know you don't have to do this, I'll speak to the clerks, you're not a bloody waitress you know"

"Ah sure its fine, it's a good way of walking up to random people and introducing myself without it seeming like naked self promotion – it totally is naked self promotion but I'm just hiding it behind champagne"

"Ok, if you're sure, but don't feel like you have to do it, there are other ways of meeting people, and to be honest, in an hour's time most people in here are going to be so pissed they won't remember their own name, let alone yours!"

"Well thanks for the vote of self confidence, and there was me thinking I'd use my Irish charm to ensure a steady supply of briefs come April"

"Perhaps you could just impress them with your legal ability instead?"

"God, you're so old fashioned" Niamh winked at Siobhan. "Anyhows, let me serve this and I'll catch you later maybe?"

"Sure, have fun, see you in a bit"

Siobhan did the rounds, she found Bev and Sally, some of her favourite CPS caseworkers, they were always up for a laugh and Bev was about to order shots from the bar

"Come on Shiv – I ent seen you in ages, have a Jaegarbomb with us"

Siobhan hated the nickname Shiv and she tried to politely decline, "That's very kind Bev, think I'll stick with the fizz if that's alright"

"Oh come on, its Christmas, how about tequila instead?"

"No, really, thanks"

Bev was the life and soul, and she could be very persuasive. "I remember your first chambers do, you got hammered and we ended up in Flares on Broad Street dancing to Come on Eileen"

Siobhan smiled at the memory, that had been a bloody good night, and so long ago now. She felt old, and tired, and boring. "Come on, make it a vodka and I'm in"

"That's my girl, 3 vodkas, luv!"

The bar man lined them up "One, two three- down it!"

Siobhan tossed it back "Eurgh. I mean thanks Bev"

She felt the vodka burning her throat, moments later Sally was ordering another round "Come on, let's make a night of it"

Fuck it thought Siobhan as she knocked back the second vodka, she felt her eyes start to water. Thirty minutes later she was on the dance floor as Oops up side your head began to blare out.

Niamh stood at the side of the dancefloor, watching, she didn't take her eyes off Siobhan.

Suddenly she felt an arm round her waist

"Niamh, how lovely to see you socially" -it was Berkshire, and he stunk of booze.

"Hello, Gerry"

"My, you're looking lovely tonight"

"Thank you"

"So, I feel I didn't really get to know you during our week together, can I get you a drink now?"

"No, I have one, thank you"

"I was always taught never to say no to the offer of a free drink, don't they teach you youngsters anything these days"

"I'm not being rude, it's just I'm fine and I have a drink, thank you."

Niamh started to walk away, Gerry put his hand on her bottom. Niamh whirled round and slapped him across the face. He staggered back in surprise. The music was still playing but the conversation stopped, all eyes were on Niamh.

"How dare you, you little bitch"

"You grabbed my arse you perv"

Julian, one of the marketing assistants came rushing over, Steve, the clerk also reacted.

"Sir, perhaps if we could talk about this"

"That little hussy just slapped me"

"He felt me up"

"Alright" cried Steve, "Come on, let's not do this in public. He began to usher Gerry away and Siobhan stepped forward, she went to Niamh's side. "Come on, Niamh, let's get some fresh air"

She could feel Niamh trembling with rage as she put her hands on her shoulders and guided her through to the beer garden, Steve meanwhile took Berkshire to the front door. Everyone parted as the two groups made their respective ways through the bar.

It was freezing outside and neither were wearing coats. "What the hell happened?"

"Berkshire tried it on, he wanted me to have a drink and when I said no he felt my arse"

"Fucking dick. Are you OK?"

"Yeah, I mean, no, not really. It's not exactly the way I wanted everyone to get to know me, 'Oh look, that's the pupil who smacked Berkshire"

"Don't you worry about that, there's been a queue of people wanting to do that for years. Look you're shivering" Siobhan took off her suit jacket and slipped it around Niamh's shoulders.

"Now you're going to freeze"

"Don't worry about me, I've got my vodka jacket on"

Niamh was still shaking. Siobhan put her arms around her to try and warm her. Niamh responded by placing her arms around Siobhan's waist. They stood in silence for a few moments, each enjoying the warmth and touch of the other. Siobhan could feel Niamh resting her head on hers, her head was closer to Niamh's chest and she could feel her heart pounding. At that moment she had never wanted to kiss anyone more. She could feel herself swaying as the alcohol began to take effect. Taking a deep breath she stepped away. "Let's get you home"

"Yeah, that'd be grand, thanks"

They walked back inside, the music was still playing and the crowd had begun chatting again, but a few people still looked over at Niamh as she walked through the bar.

Siobhan found Steve and explained she was going to take Niamh home.

"Thanks Miss, I think Mr Berkshire has left already"

"Good, and on Monday I want the Head of Group to raise this as a formal disciplinary matter"

"Yes Miss, sorry it happened"

"It's not your fault, Steve, we all know what Berkshire's like, the dinosaur should have retired years ago."

"Maybe this'll be the thing what finishes him off"

"I hope so. Look, make sure everyone has a good time, I'll speak on Monday"

"Thanks Miss, speak Monday"

Siobhan walked outside to see if she could spy any cabs, not one to be seen. What about uber, nope, typical.

"It's only about a 10 min walk to the Jewellery Quarter from here, I'll be fine"

"Oh no, you are not walking home alone, especially not after what just happened"

"Sure I'll be fine, I'm a big girl now"

"No, and that's the end of the matter. Look, I'll walk you back and try and pick up a cab from yours"

"You don't have to do that"

"Try and stop me"

They set off down Newhall Street, over the flyover and into St Paul's. It was freezing but Siobhan barely noticed the cold. As they walked past The Jam House Niamh slipped her hand into Siobhan's. This time Siobhan didn't flinch, they walked on, hand in hand, until they reached Niamh's flat.

"What about Gemma?"

"Eh?"

"Your partner, is she home?"

"Oh, right, erm, no, she has her own works thing this weekend. Will you come in for a coffee whilst you wait for a taxi?"

"Thanks, that'd be nice"

Siobhan stepped into the flat, taking it in. It was in an old factory, typical of the hundreds of flats that had been converted in this area. All of the walls had stunning cityscape photographs on them, except for the lounge which had a nude line art drawing of a woman hanging centre stage above the sofa. Siobhan stared at it, taken in by the beauty and simplicity.

There was only one bedroom as far as she could tell, and an open plan lounge diner. A desk was tucked in the corner. Everything was clean, ordered, light oak, brushed steel. The sofa was one Siobhan recognised as coming from Loaf, it was an electric blue and looked so inviting.

"I'll put the kettle on, you have a seat, unless you fancied a nightcap?"

"I wouldn't say no to a gin"

"Gin it is, I got this amazing Cotswold gin from Loki the other day, you'll love this"

Five minutes later, Siobhan had kicked her heels off and was curled up on the sofa, gin in hand. Niamh sat down next to her.

"Look, thanks for tonight, I really appreciate you stepping in like that"

"Well I was hardly going to stand by and watch was I?"

"I know, but with me being the pupil and all I don't want to cause any problems in chambers"

"Don't worry about that, people know what he's like, he's just got away with it for so long now I think he thinks he's impervious"

"I shouldn't have hit him though"

"I dunno, a little summary justice never hurt"

Siobhan took a sip of her gin, "I'm going to regret this in the morning, I should get going soon"

"You don't have to"

"Have to what?"

"Go"

Siobhan swallowed deeply, her lips felt dry and her heart was racing. Niamh leaned in towards her and kissed her on the lips, Siobhan felt her body respond and she kissed back, deeply, allowing her tongue to probe lips softer than she had ever experienced before. It was such a different feeling to kissing Danny, mind you she hadn't kissed anyone else for over 20 years, perhaps she'd forgotten what it was like. But this, it was so soft, and gentle, and also the most erotic feeling she had encountered in years.

"Stop" Siobhan gasped, she pulled away. "I can't, I'm married. This is wrong, I'm sorry"

She looked around and quickly gathered her shoes and bag, "I'll find myself a cab, thanks for the drink, but I have to go"

She almost ran out of the flat, if Niamh replied she didn't hear it, she was too busy thinking about what had just happened.

Outside she felt the cold air wash over her. She stood on the corner, heart pounding and closed her eyes.

Chapter six

Danny nudged her at 9am. "Are you getting up, Emily needs a lift into town." Siobhan opened one eye and felt a wave of dizziness wash over her. "Gimme a minute" She could feel the vodka shots repeating, this is why she didn't do shots, bloody Bev! Memories of last night came flooding back, the smell of Niamh's hair, the taste of her lip balm, she felt herself go red.

"You alright?"

"Yeah, bit of a heavier night than I was expecting that's all. Do us a favour love and put the kettle on, I'm gasping for a cuppa"

Danny traipsed downstairs and Siobhan lay in bed, her mind racing. The guilt coursed through her, how could she have kissed someone, and another woman! She had never cheated on Danny in her life, despite his faults she loved him and had never contemplated an affair, and then Niamh had waltzed into her life. What he didn't know wouldn't hurt him, he wouldn't find out, she just needed to make sure it never happened again.

Gingerly she stepped out of bed, she pulled her dressing gown tight around her and slowly walked downstairs. A cup of tea was waiting on the kitchen table, she grabbed it, gratefully, and took it through into the lounge. She sat on the sofa, curled up and silent, waiting for the tea to cool.

"Blimey, must have been a big one, you look as rough as a badger's arse"

"You're a charmer, as always"

"Bit old to be getting pissed like that aren't you love?"

"It was Bev, she made me do shots"

"Made you, what are you, a teenager?"

"Gimme a break will you, it was a Christmas bash, you know what they're like"

"Yeah well you'd better pull your finger out, Emily is meeting her friend at 10 and wants a lift"

"Why can't you take her?"

"I've promised Ben me and him will take the bikes out"

"Fine, let me finish this then I'll get dressed"

By 10.20am she was back home, she wasn't sure she should even have driven, but she had enough guilt regarding Niamh without factoring in drink driving offences too. Ben and Danny had both gone out and the house was blissfully silent. She made another cup of tea and sat on the sofa, hoping her head would stop pounding soon. Her phone buzzed.

"Are you OK?" It was Niamh.

Siobhan just held the phone in her hand, staring at the message. She didn't know what to say, or how to explain in 160 characters the turmoil of emotions she was currently experiencing. In the end she opted for the coward's way out and said nothing. She sat there in silence for another ten minutes, trying to work out what to do. Housework. That was the answer.

She knew she was punishing herself, penance in reality, but she forced herself to clean the bathrooms, then vacuum, before tackling the washing. By 1pm she was feeling a little better and even had an appetite.

Danny and Ben burst through the door. "What's for lunch Mom, I'm starving"

"How about we all go to McDonalds?"

"Yeah! Can I have a happy meal?"

"Aren't you getting a bit old for a Happy meal?"

"Oh Mom, I'm only 9!"

She picked up her car keys and they drove off. Fat, fat, and coke, that's what she needed now.

Twenty minutes later and the inevitable feelings of guilt settled in, the Big Mac finished, the last few fries lying at the bottom of the bag. To hell with it, her hangover was starting to feel better. Ben was happily playing with the latest piece of plastic tat, Dan was wiping ketchup from his chin.

"Come on Ben, you've got your trumpet lesson to get ready for. Have you practised at all this week?"

He gave a sheepish grin, "Sorry Mom, I will next week, promise"

"Hmm. Go and get your book and I'll drop you down"

With Ben at his lesson and Emily still in town it left just her and Dan in the house.

"Dan, do you fancy going out for dinner one night, just you and me?"

"Why?"

"Cos we haven't been out together in ages and I think we need to spend some time together"

He looked at her suspiciously, Siobhan could feel herself going pink.

"There's a new Italian opened up in Mere Green, meant to be really nice, I could ask my Mom to babysit"

"Yeah, I guess we could. I'm meeting the lads on Thursday though"

"So I could book for next weekend, Friday night maybe?"

"Ok. Are you alright, you seem a bit funny?"

"I'm fine, just tired"

She left it at that, not sure enough of her own emotions to know she wouldn't give anything away. She felt her phone buzz again

"Siobhan, talk to me" – Niamh again. She still didn't know what to say, or whether she should even say anything. A lifetime of dealing with criminals and knowing how text messages were saved meant she didn't want to say anything in a text that could later be used against her. She waited until Danny had disappeared into the garage then she went upstairs into their bedroom and closed the door.

The phone rang out, three, four times. No answer. Siobhan looked at the screen, unsure what to do next. It clicked onto answer phone, she didn't leave a message. She lay down on the bed and just stared at the ceiling, How the fuck did this happen? She jumped as her phone began to ring.

"Hello?"

"Hey, its me"

"Hi"

"Hey yourself. Are you ok?"

"Fine"

"You don't sound fine"

"I'm ok, tired that's all"

"I thought we should maybe talk about last night"

"Nothing happened, I was drunk, that was all"

"Siobhan, it was more than that and you know it"

"No, it was a stupid, drunken kiss, and that was all"

"Oh come on, I was there too you know, you kissed me back and you wanted more"

"No. I'm married, it was just a silly, drunken mistake, nothing more, nothing less. OK"

"Siobhan don't be like that"

"I'm not being like anything, ok, I just want to forget it happened, alright?"

"It's not as easy as that"

"Well it has to be, we have to work together, you're in a relationship too, aren't you worried?"

"I know what that kiss meant, and I know you felt it too. Siobhan at least meet me so we can talk about this face to face."

"I can't, I'm sorry. Look I've got to go. I'll see you around" She pressed "End" and sat on her bed. She noticed she was trembling again. She also knew that she badly wanted to see Niamh again, that despite every part of her knowing that what she was doing was wrong she couldn't stop thinking about their kiss. She would just have to avoid her, how hard would it be? Unless they were in the same court they would have no reason to see each other.

Resolved she got off the bed. She felt slightly dirty, ashamed, embarrassed. She had a hot shower, almost trying to wash her shame away. Feeling better she went downstairs, it was time to collect Ben, and Emily would be home soon. Time to think of the family, and not her own stupid feelings.

She threw herself into being a better mother, on Sunday she even made a cake.

"Mom this is great" Ben said appreciatively, with chocolate smeared around his mouth.

"I just thought it had been a while since I'd done any cooking"

"Not bad" – high praise indeed from Emily.

Baking complete she turned her mind to Monday's trial, dangerous driving, nothing too complicated. After a couple of hours she was done and she put the laptop away gratefully. Next, she phoned the Italian restaurant.

"I've got us a table for next Saturday, 7.30pm"

"Alright, should be nice, thanks love"

The week passed by in a blur of evidence, speeches and happy clients. Before she knew it Saturday had arrived and her Mom was at the doorstep ready to babysit.

"I don't need a babysitter Mom, I'm 12"

"I know, but Ben does, and if I leave the two of you alone I don't know if I'll have a house to come back to"

Emily flounced to her room. Siobhan let her mother in.

"Hiya Mom"

"Hiya love. Ooh put the kettle on, I'm gasping. Got any biscuits in?"

Typical, her mother continually moaned about her weight but try suggesting she perhaps didn't eat two digestives with every cup of tea and you might as well suggest she swim the Channel.

"Yeah , I'll put it on. Here, give me your coat, you go into the lounge. Dan's just getting changed."

She made her mom a cup of tea and then went upstairs to finish her make up.

"What's the occasion anyway?"

"No reason, just thought me and Dan hadn't been out in a while"

"Oh well, have a nice time. You won't be too late will you, I've got church in the morning"

"No Mom, we'll be home by 10.30pm"

The restaurant was doing a brisk trade when they got there. Siobhan felt herself relax slightly as they sat at the table.

"Do you want to share some wine?"

"Love you know I don't like wine"

"I just thought maybe we could share a bottle"

"Nah, pint for me thanks"

They ordered the drinks and sat in silence for a few minutes.

"So how was work this week?"

"Alright. Busy, this new house we're fitting out wants to work off about 3 different circuits, and the pull through of the wires has been tough"

Siobhan desperately tried to appear interested, but her mind began to wander. She just couldn't bring herself to care about electrical wires. She knew she was being unfair, her job held no interest for Dan either. She felt they were going through the motions.

"Have we sorted out where we're going to spend Christmas this year?"

It was always a bone of contention, Siobhan's Mother was on her own and wanted to spend Christmas with her family, but Dan had three siblings, all with children and they always had invites from at least one of them to spend the day there. Part of her wished they could go away, rent a nice cottage, somewhere by the sea, just the four of them but the arguments that would cause were just not worth it.

"Chris has asked us over, he's even said your Mom can come if she wants"

That was a pleasant surprise, her Mom would moan at the idea of not being in her own home, but this way she could still see the kids and they would be able to see some of Dan's family too.

"That's a good idea, I'll speak to Mom about it, but that could work"

Their food arrived and they dived in, hungrily. Siobhan drank her red and Dan moved onto this fourth pint.

"Tenerife was good last year wasn't it"

Siobhan smiled at the memory, "yeah, amazing weather. Makes you want to be there when it's like this outside" The alcohol was taking effect and they began to reminisce about holidays past. Siobhan had relaxed into the meal and Dan was doing his impressions, she was laughing at his Tommy Cooper.

"Pudding?"

"Yeah, let's go crazy. We could get a couple and share if you want?"

It was little things like that which made Siobhan remember why she had fallen in love with him, he knew she always wanted at least three different puddings from the menu so he'd order a mixture and he never minded sharing.

Chocolate brownie, salted caramel cheesecake and an espresso later and Siobhan could feel her trousers cutting into her waist. "That was good"

Dan burped, "No kidding. This was a good idea love, you know we should try and do this more often"

"We really should. We'd better get back now though, my Mom will be standing at the door with her coat on"

They caught a cab and even held hands in the cab on the way back. Siobhan couldn't help but think that the last time she had held hands with someone, it had been Niamh.

Emily was still up when they got in, Siobhan's mother was dozing on the sofa.

"Mom, we're back"

"Eh? I wasn't asleep you know"

"It's OK, we're back. Have the kids been ok?"

"yeah, though they don't half watch some rubbish on telly"

She gathered her belongings and said her goodbyes. Siobhan got Emily to bed then she and Dan finally sat down with the house to themselves.

"Fancy a nightcap?"

Siobhan flinched, the last person who had offered her a nightcap was Niamh.

"Baileys would be nice, thanks love"

She needed to calm down, her heart was thumping again, she was sure Danny could tell something was wrong.

"God, I needed that" he sipped his whisky. Siobhan smelt her Baileys, it always smelled of Christmas she thought. They finished their drinks in a matter of minutes.

"Ready for bed" Dan had a twinkle in his eye.

"I could be persuaded"

Siobhan checked in on the children, both fast asleep. She brushed her teeth and crawled under the duvet. Dan was already in bed, naked – his way of letting her know he was in the mood. She cuddled in to him, trying to remember how long it had been since they had last made love. Weeks? Surely not a month? Maybe.

It wasn't that the sex was bad, it was just – nice. There were no surprises anymore, first he would kiss her on the lips, then the neck, then he would hopefully guide her down so he could get a blow job. He was a man of simple tastes, if she was lucky she got a nipple tweak but after a couple of minutes he would climb on top, a few thrusts and that was it. She enjoyed being with him, but sometimes she yearned for a few fireworks.

Within minutes Danny was snoring next to her. Siobhan lay awake a while longer, the conversation with Niamh the previous week all she could think about.

Chapter seven

The weeks in the run up to Christmas were always insane at work, solicitors demanded urgent advices, clients expected you to get them bail so that they wouldn't have to be in prison for Christmas. The Judges were always more short tempered as the listing officers crammed cases into their courts in a desperate effort to clear an ever growing backlog. Not only did Siobhan have cases to deal with but naturally all of the preparation for Christmas fell to her too. She loved buying the kids presents but she resented the fact she had to sort out all the presents for Danny's family members too. She worked full time, just like he did, why was it always on her.

She was chuntering to herself as she battled the crowds at the Bullring, she had made the mistake of dashing out on her lunchbreak as she tried think of what to buy her Mom and Danny's Dad. If all else failed he would just get socks.

At 1.45pm she realised she was going to be late back to court if she didn't leave straight away. She looked at the items in her basket, then at the queue for the till, and gave up. She abandoned the basket in the middle of the shop floor and began to walk at breakneck speed to get back to court. She was in the middle of another rape trial and was calling her client after lunch. She dashed through security and practically ran up the stairs at Birmingham Crown court, she keyed in the code for the robing room and was just about to pull the door when it opened for her. John Evans was there, with his pupil, Niamh standing behind him.

"Ah, Siobhan, I've been looking for you"

"Really? Sorry, I was out shopping. What's up, and make it quick, I'm in front of Perkins in two minutes"

"My trial has cracked and I'm going to head off home, I'm looking for someone to take Niamh for the afternoon and the clerks said you were part heard, is it OK if she comes with you?"

Siobhan opened her mouth to say no, then realised that might look odd. "Er, fine, I've got to get my robes, Niamh go along to court 8 and I'll be there in a minute" She couldn't even look Niamh in the eye.

"Thanks Shiv, appreciate it. She's a good girl, she'll take a decent note too"

John disappeared, lucky sod getting an early bath, Siobhan thought grimly. Niamh was still standing by the door. "Go, court 8, I'll see you down there!"

Why had she snapped at her? Siobhan pulled her gown around her and was still adjusting her bands as the tannoy went "Could Miss Flaherty of counsel please make her way to court 8 immediately" Bloody Perkins, always desperate to get court started on time, she had no kids and lived for the job, she expected counsel to have the same enthusiasm.

Siobhan ran down the stairs, nearly breaking her neck as she caught her gown on the handrail. The Judge was already in court when she walked in, Niamh was sitting in the solicitor's row behind Siobhan's space.

"Miss Flaherty, are you ready to call your client?"

"Certainly, your Honour"

Her client came across well, he was a teacher accused of raping a pupil, but he was a man of good character, smartly dressed, articulate and she knew that he was making a good impression on the jury. After about an hour she had asked him all the questions she needed to, now it was the Prosecution's turn.

"Shall we take a short break before cross examination members of the jury? A chance to stretch your legs"

The court rose and Siobhan exhaled. She couldn't speak to her client now that he was in the middle of giving evidence so the safest thing to do was for him to stay in the courtroom and for her to step out.

Niamh followed behind her without being asked.

"Hi"

"Hello" Siobhan spoke stiffly, trying to be casual but coming across as stilted and awkward.

"I thought your man did well"

"Thank you, let's hope the pros don't destroy him"

"It's nice to see you"

Siobhan didn't reply. Her throat felt dry and she was struggling to act normally. She grasped around for something to say, anything, it didn't need to be cool, or witty, just something to stop this endless silence.

"I need the loo" – oh brilliant, run away from the situation Siobhan, very bloody mature.

Siobhan sat in the cubicle, she was sweating, trying to calm herself down. All this over a bloody kiss, it was amazing what a lifetime of Catholic guilt and repression could do to a person. She took a few deep breaths, and thought about what she would say when she came out. She splashed some water on her face and walked back to court 8. Niamh was still sitting outside.

"Sorry about that, I rushed back after lunch and didn't have time to go to the loo so I was desperate."

"That's fine. Thanks for letting me tag along again"

"No problem." Siobhan knew that despite her feelings of guilt she was delighted to see Niamh again. It had been two weeks, she'd hoped that memories of the kiss would have faded but just seeing her again lit a fire in her groin and brought all her emotions rushing back.

Niamh smiled at her and Siobhan gave a shy grin back.

The usher came out to call them back in, and the trial continued.

They finished for the day at 4.20pm. Tomorrow would be speeches and summing up and the jury would be out just after lunch.

"Would you mind if I came back to watch the end tomorrow, I think John only has a few bits and bobs and I'd like to try and watch more trial work if that's OK?

"Check with John, but it would be fine by me"

"Thanks. I'll message you tonight to let you know"

Siobhan stood on the busy cross city line. What did she want? She had acted like a stupid school kid today, she had to decide how to handle this otherwise she would stutter and stumble every time she saw Niamh. She knew that she had enjoyed the kiss, she couldn't deny that, but it provoked so many questions. She had never considered that she might be gay, but surely just because she had kissed one girl, one time that didn't mean she had changed. She still loved Danny, she didn't want to mess up her family. Yet she knew she had felt more emotion today than she had in weeks, she had had no excitement in her life and this, this was exciting, it was passionate, dangerous – she was wanted by someone, that desire was intoxicating and Siobhan knew in her heart of hearts that she wanted more of that attention, more of that fire inside her. Despite knowing how dangerous this could be she knew she wanted more from Niamh, but wanting something and doing something about it were two very different things, perhaps she just liked the idea of it, rather than actually going through with this. By the time she got home she felt even more confused, she felt angry with herself, this was a weakness, she needed to get a grip. And yet. She spent the evening checking her phone, waiting to see whether Niamh would be back with her tomorrow. Finally a message came through.

"Ok to be at court with you tomo x"

Siobhan cheered silently.

"Meet at 9.30 before for coffee?"

"OK. Where?"

"Boston Tea Party?"

That night as she lay in bed next to Danny she felt guilty. She knew what she was about to do and she knew it was wrong, but damn it she had spent her entire life playing it safe and thinking of others, it was time to do something for herself. No one would know, she wasn't going to tell anyone, and Niamh was in a relationship too so she had just as much to lose. This would be their own little secret.

Chapter eight

Siobhan tossed and turned all night, she knew in her heart that this was the beginning of an affair, that the vows she had made to Danny were about to be broken, but she couldn't resist the temptation, every time she thought of Niamh she felt her heart beat a little faster. It wasn't going to lead to anything, it was just going to be some passion in her life. That's what she told herself.

She was up before her alarm went off, she showered and searched for her best suit, she even put on some perfume, something she normally saved for weddings. She knew she was acting like a lovesick teenager but telling herself that was one thing, she couldn't stop the way she behaving and feeling.

She kissed Ben goodbye, then guiltily kissed Danny on the lips too "I'll see you tonight. I might take my solicitor for a drink after work, depending on how the case goes.

"Ok, I'm getting fish and chips for me and the kids so text me when you're on your way back"

Siobhan walked to the station a little quicker than normal, that flutter was still in her stomach and she had to stop herself from smiling. She was at Boston Tea Party for 9.15am, Niamh walked in shortly after.

"Can I treat you to a latte?"

"Well you sure know how to tempt a girl"

They found one of the booths in the corner, the problem with this place was that it was filled with lawyers, especially on a Friday, treating themselves to bacon and eggs before court. At least in the booth they could chat in a little more privacy.

"Look, I'm sorry I was so weird yesterday, it was just a bit of a shock seeing you"

"That's OK, I get it"

"I'm sorry I didn't reply to your texts. I didn't really know what to say"

"Well you're here now, do you know what you want to say now?"

"Not really, no" Siobhan felt awkward again, she just didn't have the vocabulary to hand to start dealing with this, so much for being an eloquent lawyer. "I just, I'm really confused. I know I like you, and that I feel funny when I see you, but I'm married, with kids, and I love them dearly and this can't go anywhere"

"Slow down. This was just a kiss, OK. I liked it too, alright? But that doesn't mean we're going to ride off into the sunset. Don't forget I'm with someone too. Let's just, you know, spend a bit more time together, and see what happens. No pressure, just two people who like each other going out for a drink or something"

"Yeah, ok, that sounds nice, I mean, I'd like that. I told Danny I was going out for a drink with my solicitor tonight, how would you feel about grabbing a drink together after work?"

"I'd like that a lot"

Niamh had this half smile, whereby she looked up almost through her hair, her dark brown eyes so inviting, Siobhan swallowed deeply. "Guess it's a date then"

"Guess so"

"We'd better get over to court, I've got a speech to make"

BY 5.45pm they were in a pub, Siobhan knew she was trying to hide from colleagues as she'd deliberately chosen a pub away from chambers. They sat in the Tap and Spire, a little bar at the back of Broad Street, Siobhan had a gin in her hand whilst Niamh had gone for white wine.

"Well done, that was a great result"

"Thanks, bit of a relief, its always worse when they've got no previous, you just feel the pressure a lot more."

"Here's to success"

They both took a drink. "I think you're amazing, in court I mean"

Siobhan smiled shyly, "I think barristers make less difference than we like to kid ourselves, juries watch witnesses, they decide who they like and who they don't like, it very rarely has anything to do with our questions or the speeches we make"

"Sure, you're just being modest now, take credit where its due, that was a bloody great speech."

"If you say so, thank you."

"I do. So, what are your plans for Christmas?"

"The usual, trying to keep all different parts of the family happy, struggling to get the kids to go to church on Christmas morning"

"I didn't know you were religious"

"Catholic, but lapsed, still, I try and make them go Christmas and Easter, plus it's not worth the grief from my mother if I don't go. How about you?"

"Religious?"

"No, I mean, Christmas plans"

"Oh, right, sorry. Yeah, I've got a flight home on the 23rd, then back on the 2nd. Spend some time with the family, catch up with old friends, you know how it is."

"Tell me about your family, I don't know much about you"

"Not much to tell. A Mammy and a Daddy, two brothers, one sister, all younger. My sister is still at home, my brothers are both away at university now so we use Christmas as a chance to get together"

"What about your partner, does she go with you?"

"Er, no, my parents aren't quite ready for me to bring a girlfriend home yet. She'll be off seeing her family away down South"

They chatted about family for a while, Siobhan felt herself relaxing, she didn't think of Danny, at home with fish and chips, or the kids with their various after school activities, for once she was just thinking of herself and what a nice time she was having. Niamh reached over and held her hand. "Would you like to maybe go on for dinner somewhere?"

Siobhan checked her watch, it was already nearly 7pm. "Let me just text Danny, but yeah, that sounds good"

"I know a great little Chinese near the Hippodrome"

7.30pm on a Friday in the theatre district, it was always going to be busy but the Chinese Niamh knew was down a little side street and they were able to get a table easily.

"Let's get the sharing platter, that way I won't get food envy when yours looks better than mine"

Spring rolls, prawn toast, duck in plum, Singapore noodles and spare ribs later Siobhan wondered if she could discretely undo the button on her skirt.

"You've got sauce on you" Niamh lent over and carefully wiped away some barbecue sauce that was on Siobhan's lip. She let her hand linger there and looked in Siobhan's eyes. "All better". Siobhan went pink and her mouth felt dry.

"You were right about it being a good restaurant" she replied lamely.

"Why don't we get a drink somewhere" Siobhan could hear the suggestive tone of Niamh's voice and she felt herself succumbing to that Irish lilt.

"I shouldn't, its already late and I only said I was going for a drink"

"Ah come on, you're late enough already, one more drink won't hurt"

Despite her better judgement Siobhan followed Niamh to a pub around the corner, the rainbow flag outside caught her eye and she felt guilt well up inside her again. If she was being honest with herself she was also excited, she'd never even been to a gay bar and here she was about to go to one with a woman she had known just a matter of weeks.

The bar was noisy and Siobhan suddenly felt very old, everyone just looked young and cool, she stood out a mile in her suit. "I'm not sure this is a good idea"

"Ah come on, it'll be a laugh"

"No, I feel really weird being here"

"Siobhan, would you just relax, come and have a drink, they do some mean cocktails"

A sex on the beach appeared on the bar in front of her along with a shot. "What's that?"

"Tequila, come on, loosen up a little"

Being told to loosen up had the opposite effect "Look, Niamh, I just wanted to go for a quiet drink, this isn't really what I had in mind. What if someone sees me and recognises me?"

"You're being ridiculous, we're just two work colleagues out having a drink in a bar that does great cocktails, hardly breaking the law now is it?" Niamh looked at her pleadingly. Siobhan felt herself weaken and she picked up the shot glass, "To work colleagues". She slammed it back, hating the burning sensation in her throat. Niamh laughed as she grimaced.

"Come on, they play some 80s cheese in the other room, you'll feel right at home there"

Come on Eileen was blasting out of the speakers and Siobhan smiled in spite of herself, she had always been a sucker for a cheesy song and before she could stop herself she was singing along to the insanely catchy chorus.

"That's more like it, now here's your cocktail"

Siobhan sipped from the large glass, trying to avoid being poked in the eye by the comedy umbrella adorning the cocktail. She couldn't remember the last time she had drank cocktails, let alone been singing along in a bar on a Friday night, she began to enjoy herself as the DJ played Human League, followed by Erasure, memories of her teenage years at Snobs and The Dome came flooding back.

She felt Niamh grab her hand, and before she could stop herself she had been pulled onto the dance floor. "I've got two left feet"

"Sure, no one is watching, just move to the music"

She was sure she was blushing under the lights but the alcohol was having the desired effect and she found herself shuffling around the dancefloor.

"You look good when you dance" Niamh leaned in towards her and put her arms around her waist, "Can I have the honour of the next dance with you?"

Tiffany's "I think we're alone now" blasted out and Niamh grabbed Siobhan and whirled her around, Siobhan couldn't catch her breath for laughing and she belted out the chorus. As the song finished Niamh pulled her closer and kissed her. This time Siobhan allowed herself to enjoy the moment, she kissed back and felt that throb again. For all she cared the pub could have fallen down around her ears, she stood in the middle of the crowded dance floor and kissed Niamh, her tongue probing her soft mouth, her arms moving from her waist down closer to her bottom. The two of them moved in rhythm and Siobhan felt Niamh creep a hand under her jacket and inside her blouse, the shock of another person's hand on her skin made her stop momentarily. She looked at Niamh, her eyes slowly acquiescing and then she kissed her again, enjoying the feeling of being touched and held.

Wordlessly they moved from the dancefloor over into a corner, Niamh pushed her up against the wall and carried on kissing her. Siobhan felt as if she was on fire and she never wanted that sensation to stop. She ran her hands through Niamh's dark hair and kissed her neck, enjoying the soft moan that escaped her lips.

"Do you want to come back to mine?" Niamh whispered

"I can't. I have to get home, I told Danny I was just going for a couple of drinks. Shit what time is it?"

"About 11?"

"Fuck!" Siobhan groped for her phone in her handbag, 3 missed calls and 7 texts, mostly along the lines of "Where are you" becoming blunter with each message.

"I'm sorry, I have to get back"

"Stay"

"I can't. There will be hell to pay as it is"

Niamh just stared at her, Siobhan looked away "Just fun, remember?"

"Just fun"

Siobhan kissed Niamh once more, but this time just a brief kiss to the lips. "I'll text you when I get home"

"Will I see you before I go back for Christmas?"

"Probably not, I've got so much on at the kids' schools, plus with work. And I don't want Danny to think anything is wrong"

"Well in that case I want a proper goodbye kiss"

Niamh stepped closer to Siobhan and slipped her tongue inside her, Siobhan could feel herself becoming wet and she drew away before she made a decision she would regret. "Goodbye Niamh, Happy Christmas"

"Happy Christmas to you too. See you in the New Year"

Siobhan sat in the taxi not quite believing what had just happened. As she pulled up at her drive she could see the downstairs lights were still on. Danny was still up.

"Where the fuck have you been? I've been texting"

"Sorry, I went out for a couple of drinks and the night just sort of ran away with us"

"I thought it was just a quiet one with your solicitor?"

"Yeah, but we had a good result in court, and you know what it's like round Christmas, there were loads of people out and we ended up going for a Chinese"

"You could have texted, I've been worried"

"Sorry". Siobhan was embarrassed about how easily the lies came, Danny didn't deserve this, she could tell he had been genuinely worried about her and she had been out with another woman. The guilt flooded over her once again. "I mean it, I'm sorry, it won't happen again" Siobhan genuinely meant it, she couldn't hurt him or her family, she had been selfish and there was no excuse for what she was doing.

"Ben got a certificate at school for his maths, he waited up to show you til he fell asleep on the sofa"

"Dan I said I'm sorry, laying on the guilt trip isn't going to help"

"He's left it on the kitchen table for you to see"

Siobhan stared at the certificate and felt like the worst person in the world.

Chapter nine

Barristers love Christmas, not for the sentimental reasons of spending time with loved ones, but because the courts close on the 23rd December and then don't open until at least the 2nd January. There are no phone calls from clerks, chasing advices, asking if you can just "nip to court for a quick mention", emails die down as most solicitors are off too. It is a chance for a proper break, guilt free because the court physically isn't open so you can't feel bad about not being at work. It's also a chance to recharge the batteries, the run up to Christmas is always so intense that most barristers become ill within a couple of days of the courts shutting.

Siobhan was no different, by Christmas Eve her throat was scratching and she couldn't stop sneezing. Danny was bringing her Lemsip refills every 3 hours and she felt fit for nothing as she lay on the sofa watching "Despicable Me 2" with Ben. Ben himself was bouncing with excitement, although he was too old to still believe in Father Christmas he knew that Christmas meant presents and he had his heart set on the new Xbox, all of his school friends had computer consoles and chatted to one another, until now Ben had only been allowed the simple console, not the chat function, but this year he had asked and Siobhan and Danny had relented. Emily just wanted clothes, which was fine, except Siobhan had no clue what was cool in the world of 12 year olds right now and she had therefore gone for the lazy option of clothes vouchers.

She couldn't face cooking so they had ordered in a pizza, she didn't even fancy a drink and by 9pm she went to bed, feeling distinctly sorry for herself.

Ben came into their room at 7am on Christmas morning, Siobhan had to peel him off the ceiling, he was so desperate to get downstairs, but they had a rule that the kids opened their presents together and at the moment Emily was still sleeping peacefully. Thankfully the long night sleep had done her good and although her nose was red and still streaming she felt better in herself. By 8am Ben couldn't be contained so Siobhan made Emily a cup of tea and woke her gently.

She loved Christmas morning, ok, it wasn't as magical now that the kids didn't believe in Father Christmas but she still adored watching them rip open their presents, the squeals of delight as they got what they wanted.

"Yes, X Box and Fifa! Thanks Mom. Can I set it up now?"

"Soon Ben, don't forget we've got to be at mass at 10.30am, and we haven't eaten anything yet"

"Oh please Mom, it won't take long"

"No, after church, besides you've still got other presents here you haven't opened"

Emily was already on her ipad, looking at clothes online trying to work out how to spend her vouchers.

"Here you go love, this is for you" Danny handed Siobhan a small box. Siobhan was surprised, she normally gave Danny a list of items with the link to the online store to buy them- that way she knew she'd get something she actually wanted, and that would fit, but this box didn't resemble anything she had asked for. She opened it gingerly, inside was the most beautiful Celtic Cross, with a small emerald at the centre. "Danny, it's gorgeous!" She didn't need to feign surprise, she was genuinely blown away by the stunning piece of jewellery. "You shouldn't have spent so much on me! We can't afford that"

"Works been really good these last few months, and I've thought you seemed a bit stressed, so this is my way of just showing you I care"

Siobhan wasn't often speechless, she didn't know what to say to Danny so she just hugged him. She felt herself welling up and the emotions she'd been repressing for the last few months were dangerously close to spilling out. "You big softie, thank you!" She searched under the tree and found the present she had wrapped for him, "Sorry, this is going to seem a bit crap now"

Danny opened the present and smiled warmly at his new jumper, if he was disappointed he didn't show it.

"Come on, better get a wriggle on, do you all want some toast just to keep us going til after church?"

They wolfed down some toast, got changed into their smart outfits and got in the car to church, it wasn't the closest one but it was where Siobhan had been going since she was a child and she knew the Priest as well as most of the congregation. She didn't go very often now, but her mother ensured that everyone knew what she was up to, and which cases she had been working on. If a case made the local paper then a copy would have been passed around the pews within a matter of days.

It felt comfortingly familiar to see the same faces, the same teenagers dragged to church for the annual ritual, and she hugged the regulars warmly.

After the Gospel the Priest began his sermon "This Christmas morning we give thanks for what we have, Jesus was born and light came into the world and for that we say Alleluia. It's important that Christmas is not just about the presents, the giving of gifts, it is also about the giving of thanks for what we have received, spiritually, emotionally. Look around the benches, look at the faces of those who love you, give thanks for that love, given by God so that we can enjoy it here on Earth.."

As he continued Siobhan looked around at her family, she felt a wave of sickness pass over her and she had to sit down. There was Danny, his arm protectively around Ben. Emily was sitting next to Siobhan's mother. They all looked so happy, and she had been on the verge of ruining it. All for a selfish moment of excitement. Enough, never again. She promised herself that was the last time, she would focus on her family now.

"You OK?" Danny whispered

"Still suffering a bit with my cold, just feel bit woozy"

Siobhan's mother shot her a look that said "You may be 44 but you still don't talk in church" and Siobhan put her head down to avoid her mother's glare.

Once mass has finished the Priest stood at the door of the church greeting the congregation as they left

"Not seen you for a while Siobhan, my haven't the children grown" She had known Father Flynn since she was a child, he had baptised both of her children and he still had the ability to make her feel guilty.

"Merry Christmas Father, lovely to see you looking so well", she dodged his rebuke and hurried out to her family. It was always enjoyable to catch up with people she hadn't seen for a while, former classmates who, like her had children of their own. She sometimes couldn't believe that the people she had played tig with in the playground now had teenage children and she had to remind herself they were no doubt looking at her the same way.

After mass they had breakfast at home, before gathering up the presents ready for the trip to Dan's brother, Chris. The car was packed but they still had to pick Siobhan's mother up.

"I can hardly breathe in here Siobhan, could you not have got a bigger car?"

"Sorry Mom, not quite on the budget this year, Ben will sit in the middle so you can have a seatbelt at least"

"Mom I'm squashed"

"Stop moaning, Ben, it's only an hour's drive"

"Eugh Ben have you farted, that's gross"

"Emily don't talk to your brother like that"

The bickering continued all the way to Shrewsbury, so much for Christmas harmony thought Siobhan.

Chris greeted the family warmly, his two girls were younger than Ben and Emily but they got on well as a family, and Sue, his wife, had some mulled wine going on the cooker.

"Can I tempt you?"

"Better not, I promised Danny I'd drive, I'll have a glass with dinner but that's all"

"Maggie, lovely to see you too"

Siobhan's mother smiled warily, she didn't really enjoy being in someone else's house at Christmas, to her mind she was always the host, but with children, in laws and grandchildren to deal with, she knew there was a time for keeping quiet. "Chris, thank you for inviting me, I got you a little something".

Chris took the bottle of red gratefully and the family piled in.

Soon the living room was filled with excited chatter as the families exchanged gifts and the children excitedly ripped off packaging. Siobhan looked around and smiled, she relaxed for the first time in days and just enjoyed watching her family having fun, cousins teasing each other, Emily trying to act like a cool teenager, but actually just as excited about Christmas as she always was.

"So what did Dan get you Siobhan?"

"This" and she showed Sue her new necklace

"Blimey, what's he done wrong that he got you that?!" Sue laughed.

"What, a bloke can't treat his wife every now and again?" Danny sounded genuinely offended.

"It's lovely, Dan, well played. Chris got me a new vacuum!"

They all laughed and the moment of tension passed.

Dinner was a success, Siobhan ate far too much, but still found time for pudding, and she knew that when the sweets came out later she'd pig herself on those too. Her trousers felt tight again and she told herself the diet would start in January. Just like it did every January.

At one point, whilst the children were playing a particular elongated game of Bingo Siobhan felt her phone buzz. She looked at it "Happy Christmas. N x" She put the phone away quickly, hoping that no on had noticed. Today was not the day to be thinking of Niamh.

By 8pm the kids were getting tired and it was time to say their goodbyes. Siobhan's mother had been pointedly looking at her watch for a good thirty minutes, about as subtle as a panzer tank.

"Thanks for having us all, its been lovely"

"You're welcome, can't believe how big your pair have got, we mustn't leave it so long next time"

They finally all squeezed into the car and Siobhan got into the driver's seat. "Belts on"

"Yes Mom" came the chorus from the back.

"Siobhan could you get a move on, I'm not feeling so grand and want to get home"

"Of course, Mom, we're good to go now"

Siobhan looked at her mother in the rear view mirror, it was dark but she thought she looked a little pale, she was also quiet, which was unusual for her to say the least. "You alright Mom?"

"Just feeling a little tired, I think I've got indigestion"

"We'll get you dropped off first"

Ben and Emily fell asleep before they even reached the M54, Dan had also started to snore in the front passenger seat.

"You were quiet today Siobhan"

"Couldn't get a word in edgeways Mom, you know how it is"

"Is everything alright with you and Daniel?" She was the only one who insisted on calling him by his full name.

"Fine, life's just busy, you know how it is"

"Always busy, rushing around here and there, you'll rush yourself into an early grave if you don't calm down. And Dan said something about you being late a few nights?"

"When he did say that?"

"Oh, just as I was talking to him about the necklace he got you. He said he felt he you were a bit distant lately and he was worried he hadn't been looking out for you, and then he mentioned that you'd been out with solicitors"

Siobhan looked across at Danny, he seemed to be fast asleep. "You know what it's like at Christmas Mom, there are loads of parties and things going on so I've just been at a couple of those"

"Just don't be taking a fella for granted, you're not that much of a catch you know Siobhan"

She always knew how to make her feel useless. "Thanks Mom."

They sat silently for a short time.

"Is there something you need to tell me Siobhan?"

"Don't know what you mean Mom"

"I know you, you're not telling me something"

"Mom, just leave it will you" Siobhan didn't mean to snap but she couldn't help herself. Her Mom could always see right through her.

"I just worry about you Siobhan, that's all"

"I'm ok, Mom, been working hard, crime isn't getting any easier, and the fees keep being cut so I feel I'm just treading water even though we're expected to do more and more."

"There's something else Siobhan, what's going on with you?"

"Nothing Mom, honestly" Siobhan felt herself going red, she hated lying to her Mom but at the same time she knew she couldn't tell her the truth, it would break her heart, and destroy her family, and much as she had enjoyed the attention from Niamh the risks were too great, and the consequences were it all to go wrong, just too awful to contemplate. She looked back to her Mom and tried to give her a reassuring smile, she knew it looked fake but it was the best she could do.

They pulled up at her Mother's house just before 9.30pm. Everyone woke up as the car engine went silent.

"I'm just going to take Mom in, be back in a sec"

Siobhan helped her mother out of the back and got her house keys out of her handbag. The house felt cold as she opened the door. "Let me put the fire on"

"Don't fuss child, I grew up in a time before central heating you know"

"I know Mom, but its Baltic out there, I don't want you to catch a cold"

"I'm boiling Siobhan, go on, get yourself home. I'm going to get myself a Bovril and have an early night"

"Alright, just take care of yourself, I'll give you a call tomorrow and let you know what time I'll pick you up. Thanks for the presents Mom, I've had a lovely day"

"God Bless Siobhan, and you look after that fella of yours"

"Yes Mom"

She returned to the car and watched her Mom lock the door, she saw the landing lights go on and knew her Mom was getting ready for bed.

"Right kids, home then bed, it's been a long day"

The house was cold and dark when they got in, Siobhan turned on the Christmas lights, and the fire in the lounge. Once the children were in bed she got herself a Baileys, Danny poured himself a large measure of whisky and they sat in companionable silence in the lounge. Siobhan felt herself falling asleep on Danny's shoulder. She felt so safe when she curled up against him, his muskiness was familiar and comforting, he felt strong, her protector.

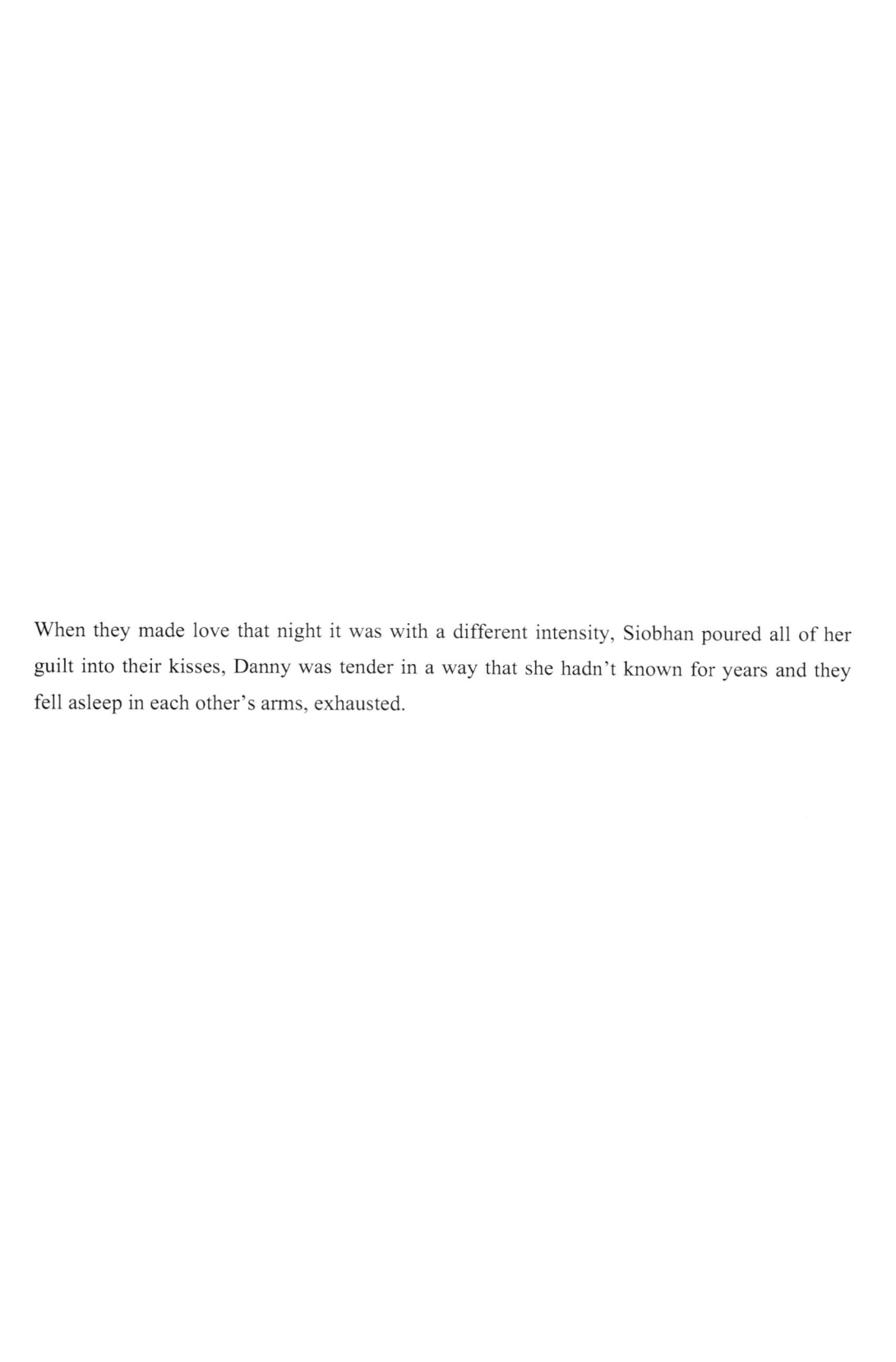

When they made love that night it was with a different intensity, Siobhan poured all of her guilt into their kisses, Danny was tender in a way that she hadn't known for years and they fell asleep in each other's arms, exhausted.

Chapter ten

Siobhan loved Boxing Day, no rush to get up, an excuse to spend as much time as possible in pyjamas and to indulge in the Christmas chocolate. The children were happily playing with their new toys, or browsing online looking at new clothes in Emily's case, and Siobhan had time to just sit quietly with a book and a cup of tea. Heaven.

At 11.30am she picked up the phone to call her Mother, if they hadn't had Christmas Day at hers then Siobhan would prepare a Christmas tea and they would play daft games like Bingo and charades. She just needed to check what time her mother needed picking up at.

The phone rang out. That was odd, perhaps her Mom was on the loo? Siobhan left it 15 minutes and then called again. Still no answer.

"Dan Mom isn't picking up the phone"

"She's prob on the toilet isn't she?"

"I've tried twice already, do you think she's Ok?"

"Yeah, she'll be fine. Stop worrying. Give it a few more minutes and then try again. Have you rung the mobile too?"

"No, just the landline, I'll give the mobile a try"

Still nothing. Siobhan tried again. By 12.30pm she was seriously worried. "Dan I'm going over. You stay here with the kids. I'll take my keys"

Siobhan drove the short journey to her mother's house, she felt a knot in her stomach that wouldn't go away. When she pulled up outside the curtains were still drawn downstairs, her mother always opened the curtains. "Standards, Siobhan, a woman needs standards". Siobhan could hear the voice in her head. Trying to control her breathing she opened the front door.

"Mom?" Silence. Siobhan walked through into the living room, in her heart of hearts she knew what she was expecting but if she accepted that reality she thought she might collapse.

There was no sign of her mother downstairs, Siobhan knew she had to go upstairs but she couldn't trust her legs to carry her safely. She called out again, hopefully, futilely. Silence greeted her. Siobhan pushed open her mother's bedroom door and her fears became reality. Her mother was in bed, and if she hadn't known better Siobhan could have sworn she was sleeping, but her chest wasn't moving, and her skin had taken on a grey pallor that meant only one thing. The strength went from Siobhan and she collapsed to the floor. She tried to cry but no sound would come.

She didn't know how long she had been sitting there when she felt her phone buzzing. It was Danny.

"Siobhan, everything ok?"

She tried to speak but still the words wouldn't come. How do you say something like that, saying it out loud would make it real and she wasn't sure she was ready for that.

"Siobhan?" She could hear the urgency in his voice.

"Dan" it was all she managed to say, but he knew.

"Oh God. Siobhan stay there, I'll be as quick as I can"

Siobhan sat looking at the phone, dumbly. What did she do? There was no point calling an ambulance, it was past that, she didn't need to call the Police, or did she? It wasn't suspicious. Who were you meant to call in this situation? Her brain wasn't functioning as it normally would. She managed to stand up, and acting almost on auto pilot she pulled the bedclothes over her mother's face, that's what you did right? You covered the face, gave the dead dignity? Yet when she looked at her Mom covered up like that it felt as if she was trying to hide her away, it looked wrong, and Siobhan pulled the cover back again, feeling that sickness once more when she saw the colour of her Mom's skin, the essence of her now gone.

She was disturbed by the sound of the doorbell. How long had she been standing there? She heard the sound of Danny coming upstairs. As he walked through the bedroom door she threw herself at him and finally the tears came. They stood there, Siobhan sobbing into his shoulder, Danny feeing utterly helpless.

Finally Siobhan found the strength to speak, "Dan, I don't know what to do. I don't even know who I'm meant to call. I just, I just don't know"

"It's alright love, we'll work it out, come on"

He led her from the bedroom, sat her in the lounge and went to make a cup of tea. Siobhan felt numb, her father had died years ago after a long battle with cancer, long enough ago that the pain had subsided, and by the end he had been in so much pain that death was a relief;

this felt different, more raw, unexpected. She had no brothers or sisters, it was just her and her Mom, and now, nothing.

Dan came in from the kitchen holding a mug of tea "I put three sugars in, it's meant to be good for shock"

"Thanks. Where are the kids, what have you told them?"

"I left them in front of the TV, just told them I had to go and check on something"

"How do we tell them, it will ruin Christmas"

"One step at a time. I've googled who we're meant to call and it says we should call the police and ambulance cos it was unexpected, then they can put things in motion with the Coroner"

"Ok" Siobhan felt confused, she always took care of the legal and financial matters at home, and yet, here she was unable to function, doubting herself at every turn.

"I'm going to call them now"

He went out of the room and Siobhan could hear the low murmur of his voice.

When the ambulance arrived there were no sirens, no flashing lights, it wasn't an emergency was it?

Siobhan couldn't stop the tears as the paramedics lifted the covered stretcher into the back of the ambulance.

"As it's an unexplained death we'll take her to the Coroner, then once the body has been released she'll go to whichever funeral director you're using. Here's a leaflet that explains it all a bit better."

Siobhan thanked him and watched as the ambulance drove away. She looked around the house where her mother had lived for so many years, all of her trinkets in the cabinets, her favourite chair with the indent. This wasn't happening, not her Mom, it couldn't.

"Do you need to call anyone love?"

"Erm, yeah, I need to speak to the Priest and then start letting her friends know. She still has some relatives in Ireland, I think Mom had a phone book somewhere, let me find it"

As she searched around she found one of her mother's cardigans over the back of the settee, she picked it up and inhaled deeply, it had her mother's scent ingrained in it, and Siobhan collapsed once more.

It was an hour before they got back home, the kids were still engrossed in the tv and their tablets.

"Ben, Emily, can you turn the TV off, we need to talk to you"

"Oh Mom, this is the best bit"

"Now Ben!" She hadn't meant to shout but she couldn't stop herself. Ben jumped and looked closely at his mother, he saw the redness of her eyes and this time he reached for the remote without complaint.

"I'm so sorry. I went over to Gran's place today to pick her up to come over, and when I got there. I mean, I went in. The house was quiet" Siobhan took a breath, she was struggling to get the words out, she looked at the expectant faces of her children and steeled herself. "I'm sorry, but Granny was in bed, I thought she was sleeping but she wasn't. Granny's died."

It took a few moments for the news to sink in, Emily was the first to react. "Noo! No, it can't be true. You're wrong!" Siobhan said nothing, she just pulled her children tight and let them cry their hearts out.

The rest of the day passed in a blur of phone calls, and tears. Every time Siobhan had to tell someone new she found herself having to comfort them. She felt resentful, they hadn't lost a mother like she had, how dare they be upset – this was her pain, her grief, how could they be feeling what she was feeling.

By 9pm she felt exhausted, she couldn't bear the thought of speaking to anyone else. She suddenly realised she hadn't eaten all day, but then again she felt no hunger. Dan came in with a glass of wine "Thought you might need this"

She took it gratefully and took a long drink. This was so unfair, her Mom had worked so hard all her life, she'd only been retired a few years and had so many hobbies, and clubs she went to. Bingo on a Wednesday, Social club on a Thursday, coffee mornings at church. What was the point of working so hard and saving your entire life when at the end of it all you got just a few years of freedom. Siobhan felt bitter, but at the same time emboldened. Life was for living, you couldn't look back and regret what you hadn't done. She felt the wine taking effect. "Dan I just have to make one more phone call"

"'K,"

Siobhan took herself upstairs, shut the bedroom door, and phone Niamh's number. 3 rings, 4. She nearly hung up, then that the familiar voice answered.

"Hey there"

"Niamh" she whispered the word.

"What's up, what's wrong?"

"Niamh. I. Erm. It's my Mom, she died and I don't know what to do or who to talk to but I just felt I needed to hear you. I need to feel something"

"One sec"

Siobhan could hear the sound of movement as Niamh moved from one room to another, then the sound of a door shutting.

"God Siobhan, I'm so sorry. Are you on your own, where's your family?"

"Dan's downstairs, the kids are asleep. I just needed to talk to someone and I didn't know who else to call. I'm sorry"

"That's Ok, I'm here. What happened?"

"She said she wasn't feeling great yesterday, and I just thought she was tired. I went round to hers this morning and there she was. They may have to do a post mortem because it was unexpected, but she was 70 and the paramedics said it looked like maybe a stroke or a heart attack in her sleep. I just feel so lost, and lonely. It's my Mom" Siobhan couldn't stop herself from crying then, Niamh just let the tears come.

Chapter eleven

Siobhan woke early the following morning, she looked down and realised she'd fallen asleep in her clothes. Her mouth felt dry, and she saw an empty red wine glass on the dressing table next to her.

She tried to get off the bed without disturbing Dan. She stripped off yesterday's clothes and pulled on her pyjamas and dressing gown and went downstairs. Everyone else was still asleep and she relished the silence. She felt calmer than the previous day, the fear had been replaced with just a deep sadness. She made herself a fresh cup of tea and sat on the sofa, just staring into space. Her mind flashed back to the phone call with Niamh. Although she hadn't been physically able to comfort her just hearing Niamh's voice had calmed her in a way Danny hadn't been able to. Sure, Dan had been there for her, but in a very practical, masculine way, making calls, sorting out details. Niamh had been there for her emotionally. The guilt that she had felt in church on Christmas Day seemed a life time away, Siobhan had needed something more than she was getting and Niamh could provide that. She also thought of her mother, of a life of obedience, and hard work, and where had it got her? A few years retirement, and that was it. Siobhan felt a different perspective take hold in her, one where she wouldn't look back in years to come and regret not grabbing life when she had the chance. It didn't mean that she would ever leave Dan, or the kids, but surely she deserved happiness and fulfilment? All of these thoughts tumbled around inside her as her family slept on. By the time they woke up Siobhan had already decided that she would be seeing Niamh again.

Siobhan felt disconnected from reality for the rest of the Christmas holidays, just when she needed the distraction of throwing herself into work the courts were closed. She drifted around the house, occasionally having a mad burst of energy and cleaning out some long-forgotten wardrobe. Other times she sat curled up on a chair, feeling no desire to move or to speak.

There was no date for the funeral, she couldn't even register the Death for a number of days as Council offices were closed. The Coroner had carried out a preliminary investigation, the post mortem had shown a heart attack, a strong one that would have killed her instantly. Siobhan took some comfort from that, if you were going to die, dying in your sleep in your own bed was not a bad way to go.

The earliest date they could fix the funeral for was 11th January. It felt a lifetime away. Next year. Siobhan felt in limbo and she knew she wouldn't be able to move on until her mother was buried beneath 6 feet of earth.

"Do you want to do anything for New Year?"

She looked at Dan in disbelief. "Do you really think I feel like celebrating?"

"No, but I thought it might do you good to get out, Mark and Emma down the road are having a few people over and I thought we could maybe have a few drinks. The kids could come so we wouldn't have to worry about getting a babysitter"

Siobhan just shook her head. Dan stood there awkwardly. "Would it be ok if I went? You know, just for a few pints?"

"Yeah, fine, whatever".

Siobhan felt angry, how could he feel like having fun at a time like this? She took herself into their bedroom and found an old Agatha Christie novel, her go to author when she needed to escape for a little while.

She wasn't sure how long she had the book open on her lap for, she certainly hadn't turned the page in a while, she was finding it hard to concentrate. In the end she gave up and closed the book, she looked at her watch, 10.20pm. Well this was going to go down as one of the worst New Year's Eves in history. Her phone lay beside her. She knew she shouldn't but she couldn't stop herself as she picked it up and started to type.

"Hope you're out celebrating somewhere x"

She pressed send and held her breath. Nothing. She kicked herself for feeling like this but she felt so lonely and just wanted to hear a friendly voice.

After half an hour she gave up and went downstairs in search of a drink, she found an open bottle of red and poured herself a large glass. She drank it in just a few gulps, but felt no better for it. She searched in the cupboard, thank God, there was still some gin left. She made a home measure, heavy on the gin, light on the tonic, and took it back up to their bedroom. She'd left her phone upstairs and her heart leaped when she saw she'd received two messages

"Hi, long time no hear?" followed by "How are you? x"

"Not great. Couldn't face NY celebration"

"Sorry to hear that. At family bash. Want me to call? X"

At that moment Siobhan wanted more than anything to hear Niamh's voice, to have someone to listen to her so she could talk about the rage inside her, the emptiness, but she also didn't want to talk to Niamh and hear the sound of people having fun in the background.

"It's ok, text is fine for now. Have you had a nice break? X"

"Not so bad, family driving me mad, looking forward to coming back over x"

"I'm looking forward to getting back to work, is that mad? I just need a distraction x"

"Totally understand, all you can do at the moment is sit and grieve, but til funeral takes place you will feel in limbo. X"

Siobhan held her phone, Niamh just understood, she did feel in limbo, her life couldn't move on until she had stood over her Mom's grave and said her final goodbyes. She needed work to feel some semblance of normality. She also needed to see Niamh again.

"When are u back? X"

"Fly in on the 2nd. You free for a meet up? X"

"Definitely, give me a call when you're back x"

"Will do. You take care now x"

"Thanks, will do x"

Siobhan felt better for having messaged. She looked at her watch again, nearly midnight. Her gin glass was empty so she went downstairs for a refill. Out of habit she flicked on the tv and turned to Jools Holland, the cheer in the studio was not something she was feeling herself but it was nice to have some background noise to end the silence in the house. She watched as the audience counted down and then took a long slug of gin. At 12.10am she turned the tv off and went to bed, alone.

She was awake by 8am the following morning, her head throbbing slightly, but she knew it would be nothing compared to Dan's hangover. He'd come in sometime after 3am, doing that thing only the very drunk do of trying to be as quiet as possible whilst actually sounding like an elephant stomping around the room. He was snoring heavily now, the room smelt of stale farts and Siobhan was desperate to leave and get some fresh air.

She went downstairs, and made herself a cup of tea and waited for the rest of the family to stir.

It was gone eleven by the time Danny surfaced, Siobhan had emptied the dishwasher, cleaned the cupboard under the sink and even sorted out the fridge.

"Good night was it?"

"Yeah, we went back to one of the lad's and carried on drinking. I feel dog rough"

Siobhan didn't say anything but he looked dog rough too.

"Want a bacon sandwich?"

"yes please love"

She set about making bacon and eggs, the smell soon attracted Ben and Emily and within a matter of minutes they were all wolfing them down.

"I've got a short hearing tomo in Leamington"

"Eh? I thought you were going to take some time off til the funeral"

"It's only a short case, plus I think it'll do me good to get out the house"

"Are you sure you feel up to it?"

"Yeah, the more I sit round here the worse I feel, least if I'm at work it'll give me something else to think of instead of worrying about writing the eulogy for mom."

Dan didn't say anything further, he just concentrated on eating his sandwich.

"I might see who is at court and maybe go for lunch with them?"

"Ok, it'll prob do you good to see some of your friends"

Siobhan didn't say that she hoped fervently that Niamh would be at court, or at least somewhere where they could meet for lunch. Instead she tidied up and busied herself with more housework.

Niamh texted her just after 7pm. "Landed, back at flat. How are you? X"

"Been better. Are you in court tomo? X"

"John not back til Monday so waiting to see where clerks send me x"

"I've got bits and bobs in Warwick if you want to join me? X"

"Yes please x"

"See you at 10. Oh, and it's called Warwick Crown court but it sits in Leamington, just in case you haven't been there before x"

"And they say the Irish are daft! See you tomo x"

Siobhan smiled to herself, the pleasure she felt at the idea of seeing Niamh again outweighed the guilt she had been feeling, something had changed with the death of her mother, she had a new desire to not spend her life regretting chances missed. Besides, she would be careful, no one would find out and her family wouldn't get hurt.

She was awake before her alarm and took a little extra time choosing her suit, she even put some perfume on. Her eyes had dark rings under them but she felt happier than she had done since Boxing Day.

Niamh was already at court when she arrived, Siobhan resisted the temptation to hug her, she wanted to feel her arms around her, to smell her hair but they were in the middle of the robing room and the most that she could get away with was a gentle touch to the arm and a "Nice to see you, Happy New Year"

"Likewise"

The robing room wasn't particularly busy, all new trials were starting the following Monday so the courts were just filled with mentions and sentences. Only 2 of the courts were sitting.

"I've got to find Probation, go through the report with the client and then we'll let the usher know that the case is ready"

The case went smoothly enough and by 12.15pm her client was walking out of the door, happy with his suspended sentence.

"I think we've earned lunch don't you"

"Yep, I'm famished, all I did over Christmas was eat, finding it hard to believe I'm only allowed 3 meals a day now"

"There's a lovely little tea room overlooking the park, come on, let's go there"

The tea room was quiet, not many hardy fools in the park in early January. They ordered and found a corner table.

"It's so good to see you again Niamh, I really missed you"

"You too. Now honestly, how are you?"

Siobhan hadn't meant to but she couldn't stop herself, she burst into tears. Niamh put her arms around her and just held her. The sobs wracked her body and she was struggling to breathe.

"Siobhan, breathe through your nose, in for 8, then out through the mouth for 8, 1,2,3,4, that's it"

Siobhan began to take control of her breathing again and slowly her cries subsided.

"I'm so sorry, I don't know what came over me"

"No need to apologise, you have just lost your mother you know"

"I just, I thought I was doing better, and then when you asked me how I was, I couldn't even reply. I'm not ok, I miss her so much and I don't understand what happened, I just wasn't ready for this"

"Losing a loved one is one of the most painful things you can through, but its also stressful, the body doesn't know how to process the trauma, so you react in different ways"

"You sound like you know what you're talking about"

"Trust me, I do"

Niamh ordered Siobhan a hot, sweet tea and Siobhan drank it gratefully.

"How was your break?"

"Better than yours. Good, saw my family, but I've seen enough of them now to do me for a few months. Caught up with some friends and that, usual stuff really"

"I've got a week to write my mom's eulogy, how do I put into words her life and do it justice?"

"You're a barrister, you talk for a living, you can do this. I could help you know?"

"You didn't know her"

"No, I know, but you could tell me what she was like, and between us we could turn that into something beautiful. Maybe come over to mine one night next week and we can prepare it?"

"What about Gemma?"

"She's still away til Friday"

"I'd like that, a lot"

Niamh took Siobhan's hand and held it, wordlessly. Siobhan looked at Niamh and felt the tears come to her eyes again. She swallowed deeply and tried to control her breathing again.

"Thanks, I mean that"

By the end of lunch Siobhan had even found herself laughing, something she hadn't done in a while.

"I'd better get back home, the kids are still off school and I need to sort dinner"

"Ok, what night do you want to meet next week?"

"Could you do Tuesday? That gives me time to think about what I want to say, and then still add to it before the funeral next Friday"

"Tuesday at mine, come over for 7.30pm and I'll cook something too"

They stood, Siobhan hugged Niamh once more, she had a quick glance around but the only person in the tea room was the bored assistant who was counting the coffee bags behind the counter. Siobhan leaned in and kissed Niamh, feeling once more their tenderness. She welled up again and held Niamh tighter, not wanting the moment to end.

Chapter twelve

Siobhan found herself counting the days until Tuesday. She had told Dan that she was meeting a friend to go over her mother's eulogy. It wasn't a lie, she had told herself, she was going to write it with Niamh's help. Who was she kidding, not giving the Dan the full details was exactly the same as lying.

She spent a while looking through her wardrobe, it seemed to consist of either cheap suits, or shapeless sportswear, the reality was she went out so little these days she didn't even have any decent 'going out' type tops to wear. In the end she settled on a sleeveless polo neck and some black trousers, at least black was forgiving, she could try and hide some of the excess Christmas weight.

With a tinge of guilt, she kissed Ben good night, and popped her head around Emily's door. Emily was, as usual, glued to her phone, engaged in deep snapchat conversations with her friends. "Just off to meet a friend, I'll see you in the morning"

"Bye" Emily had become even more uncommunicative since the death of her Grandmother, Siobhan had tried talking to her, in an effort to get her to open up, but Emily had shown no signs of wanting to confide in her mother. Siobhan pulled the door to and walked downstairs. Dan was in the lounge, beer in hand. "I'm off, not sure what time I'll be back so don't wait up"

"Where are you meeting again?"

"Oh, some bar in the Jewellery Quarter" Another lie, falling easily from her lips. Siobhan noticed Dan's phone on the arm of the chair. She quietly picked it up and went into the "Find my phone app". She and Dan had always had the app and used it to check on each other and what time they could expect to be home. Siobhan went to her phone and clicked "Stop sharing location", when the notification came up on Dan's phone she clicked "OK" before putting the phone back where she had found it. The last thing she wanted was for him to idly check which bar she was in and find out she was actually in a block of flats, this way, if he decided to check and noticed they weren't following she could at least blame it on a technical problem with the phone. She was ashamed of her own subterfuge, but it didn't stop her.

She walked to the train station, for once the cross city line was on time and she pulled into New Street just after 7.10pm, it gave her time to walk up to Snow Hill and catch the Metro, taking the two stops to Jewellery Quarter. She passed a Tesco on route to the flat and picked up a bottle of Merlot, then at the last minute she grabbed a bunch of flowers that was by the till. She felt like a schoolgirl about to go on her first date and she could actually feel herself trembling as she pressed the intercom button.

"Hey, push the door and come on up"

Siobhan walked into Niamh's flat for a second time, this time it felt different, she had made an active choice as to what she was about to do and although her stomach was in a tight knot she also felt the tingle of excitement.

"Good to see you, come on in"

"Thanks, should I take my shoes off?"

"If you wouldn't mind, only its wooden floors and the fella downstairs can be a bit grumpy about the noise sometimes"

Siobhan cursed herself for not wearing just plain black socks, instead she felt her cheeks redden as Niamh noticed her Minnie Mouse socks.

"Now that's not what I expected"

"Christmas present, pretty much the only pair I've got that don't have holes in them!"

Niamh laughed, but not in an unkind way, and Siobhan felt herself relax a little.

"Come on through, I'm just finishing off the dinner"

Niamh looked stunning, in a white silk blouse and leather leggings which emphasised her slim figure. Siobhan looked at her longingly.

"Smells good, whatever it is"

"Nothing fancy, just a curry"

Siobhan walked through, noticing more this time now that she was a little less drunk. She was struck once again by the art on show, and felt embarrassed by the bland Ikea prints that adorned her walls.

"Wine?"

"Yes please, oh and these are for you" she nervously handed over the wine and flowers. Niamh took them, put them on the table, then pulled Siobhan towards her. Siobhan closed her eyes and allowed herself to be consumed by Niamh. The relief at knowing there was no one watching, that she wouldn't get caught, was overwhelming and Siobhan kissed Niamh more intensely than she ever had before. Before she could stop herself, she was pulling at Niamh's blouse, and reaching for her breasts. Niamh wasn't wearing a bra and Siobhan felt her nipples harden as she caressed them. She had never touched any woman's breasts, other than her own and she was shocked at how smooth they felt, but also how excited she herself was. Her breathing was becoming shallow and she felt herself getting light headed. Niamh pulled Siobhan's top over her head, she felt exposed as she stood there with just her bra and trousers on. Niamh pulled away from kissing her and stood there for a time just staring, Siobhan felt embarrassed and crossed her arms her chest.

"Don't, I want to see you"

Siobhan looked up shyly

"You don't know how beautiful you are do you?"

Siobhan just giggled "Don't be daft"

Niamh pulled Siobhan's arms away, then gently she reached around and unhooked Siobhan's bra. Siobhan was conscious of her breasts in comparison with Niamh's, she had borne two children, breast fed them, and she felt every one of her 44 years. Yet none of that seemed to trouble Niamh, she was looking at her in a way no one else had done in a long time, she felt wanted, desired, and it was overwhelming. Niamh reached out and brushed her hand across Siobhan, Siobhan felt herself react, her nipples stiffened and she wanted to be touched more than she ever had before.

Niamh kissed her again and they stumbled to the sofa, Niamh pushed Siobhan down and her tongue began to explore her mouth, breasts, neck. She began to pull the zip of Siobhan's trousers.

"Woah, slow down"

"It's Ok, Siobhan, relax"

"This is just, God it's amazing, but this is all new, and I just need to slow down"

"Sorry, yeah, its Ok" Niamh kissed her on the mouth again and caressed Siobhan's breasts. Siobhan moaned and felt her pelvis move against Niamh's. Her body was reacting in a way that was alien to her, her head was spinning with emotion, she knew what she wanted but she was so very scared of letting herself want it so much. She pushed Niamh away.

"Perhaps, perhaps we should have something to eat, and maybe a drink, maybe talk about this"

"Is this what you do? Talk and think?"

"It's kind of who I am"

"You have to live for the moment Siobhan, enjoy what life offers, surely losing your Mom has made you realise life is short"

"Don't, don't, do that, don't make this about my Mom"

"I'm sorry, I didn't mean to offend you. I just meant that perhaps you understand now I don't want to waste time or opportunities"

"I don't, but this is all new to me, for God's sake I'm a married woman and I'm having an affair with you, just let get my head around it, alright?"

"Sorry, look, let's have a drink, the dinner is nearly ready. We can just talk if that's what you want"

"Thanks, it is"

They dressed in an awkward silence, Niamh poured Siobhan a large red and she took it gratefully. Siobhan felt her breathing begin to return to normal and she looked over to Niamh.

"I just need you to understand that what's happening here isn't something I'd ever planned, or even thought about. I love Danny, I love my kids, and I'm risking so much here, but I like you, I really like you, I just need to take this slow Ok?"

"Ok. Perhaps I can tempt you with my cooking skills instead"

Niamh plated up the hot curry and the two of them sat at Niamh's small table.

"So have you written anything for your Mammy yet"

"I've got some ideas in my head but nothing in writing yet"

"Tell me about her"

"There's a lot to say. She came over here with her parents and siblings when she 12. There was a fairly large Irish community in Erdington and they managed to get some lodgings in a small terrace with two other families. Her Dad found work in one of the factories, her Mom stayed at home to raise her and her brothers and sisters. Her Dad died in an industrial accident when she was only 17, so she had to leave school and get a job to help support her family. She was bright you know, but she never had the chance to go to university or anything to prove herself, and I think she regretted that. She made sure that I worked hard to pass the 11 plus to get the education that she never had."

"What did she do for a living?"

"She cleaned to start with, then she got work in a supermarket and then she managed to go to night school and learn to type so she worked as a secretary. I felt like sometimes, even though she wanted me to do well, she was jealous of the opportunities that I had. Not that she'd tell me one way or another how she felt"

"Typical of that generation, don't talk about feelings"

"Yeah, but then when the kids came along she was so proud. She spoilt them rotten, gave them all the things she couldn't afford to give me when I was growing up"

"Did she never want more children?"

"Oh they tried, but after me she had a couple of miscarriages and it just never happened for them again. She threw herself into the church, helping do the flowers, and run the jumble sales. She'd be the first to volunteer, and the last to leave. She never complained either, she saw it as her duty to the church"

"I think you've got yourself the start of a decent eulogy right there"

Niamh topped up Siobhan's glass, they had almost finished the red.

"I can't believe she's gone. She worked so hard all her life, and now, when she finally had time to stop and enjoy it all, it's gone." Siobhan began to cry as the pent up emotion of the last few days poured out of her. Niamh held her and let her cry. "I miss her so much"

"I know, come on, let it out"

Slowly the sobs subsided, Niamh held Siobhan's face, tilted it towards her and kissed her once more. This time Siobhan allowed herself to be kissed, their tongues probed one another's mouths and Siobhan savoured the tender, warm touch. They took it more slowly, she unbuttoned Niamh's shirt, feeling every inch of her body. She removed her own top, and then unbuttoned her trousers. She stepped out of them and let Niamh gaze upon her.

Niamh kissed Siobhan's neck, then her breasts, she knelt down before Siobhan and kissed the stretch marks of her stomach, the scar of her c-section. Siobhan felt safe, and wanted. Taking her by the hand Niamh led Siobhan into the bedroom and lay her down.

"You are the most beautiful person Siobhan, I wish you could see that"

Siobhan couldn't reply, her heart was hammering too quickly and her mouth was dry

"These scars, these scars are your story, they make you who you are and you don't need to hide them" Niamh pulled the top of Siobhan's pants down and worked her tongue slowly across the length of her scar, Siobhan felt her muscles twitch as they reacted to her touch.

Niamh removed her own trousers and took Siobhan's hand, she placed it at the top of her groin and allowed Siobhan to feel the contours of her body, her fingers probing in a way she was not used to.

"We can take this as slow as you need, but I want you Siobhan Flaherty"

Siobhan nodded and she allowed Niamh to remove her underwear, this was the first time in 15 years she had been naked before anyone except her husband or a Doctor and she felt self conscious again, her hand moving protectively over her pelvis. Niamh pulled it away and kissed her once more. Then for the first time in her life Siobhan had a woman go down on her. It was unlike anything she had ever experienced, a soft tongue that licked, gently at first, then harder as it reach her clit. Niamh took her time and Siobhan could feel the orgasm building, the kisses and licks causing her to tremble. When she came it was a release that flooded her body.

"Oh my God!"

Niamh just smiled, and kissed her scar once more, "Welcome to the dark side"

Siobhan pulled Niamh towards her and kissed her deeply, it felt odd to taste her own scent on another woman's lips. "I don't know if I can return the favour just yet, I don't feel quite ready"

"That's ok, give me your hand"

Niamh took Siobhan's hand, she interlaced their fingers and guided it down to her groin, she moved Siobhan's hand in a circular motion over her mound, Siobhan let herself be guided until, growing in confidence, she moved her fingers slowly and let them push against Niamh, her finger finding the entrance to her body and then gently pushing in and out. She could feel Niamh's wetness and knowing that she was responsible for it made her feel even more sexy and alive. The pushing grew faster, she slipped another finger inside and Niamh began to pant, Niamh pulled her closer, encircling her wrist with her hand, causing Siobhan to pump harder, harder until Niamh too came in a shattering climax.

They lay silently on the bed together, Siobhan not quite believing what had just happened.

"That was surreal"

"Well I've had better descriptions"

Siobhan laughed, "Sorry, I mean, I've never felt like that before, it was intense, and then just feeling you, being inside someone, I just, it was something else!"

"Only a woman knows how to be tender with another woman, men don't feel the same way we do, they're not sensual, or alive to the touch of the human body. Trust me, Siobhan, you'll never want sex with a man again"

"Steady on, I am still married, remember, And we talked about this, I'm not going to leave Dan, or jeopardise my relationship with my children, I thought you understood that"

Niamh looked offended, "I do understand, but I thought you enjoyed that?"

"I did, it was amazing, but you and I are both in relationships, we have to accept this for what it is, two consenting adults having some fun, but it can't go beyond that!"

"So where are we going with this?"

Siobhan was confused, "Niamh, we're not going anywhere, I thought we were just enjoying what we have, whatever is going on here"

Niamh turned away, Siobhan leaned over and pulled her towards her "This is all new for me, don't get me wrong, I like you, a lot, but we aren't just thinking about ourselves here, you have Gemma, I have Dan, we can't just ride off into the sunset and leave all that behind"

Siobhan saw a tear rolling down Niamh's cheek, she moved closer and kissed it away. Niamh looked away at first, then turned to face Siobhan. She kissed her once again and Siobhan felt her body responding. They pressed together and no more was said.

Siobhan awoke with a start, she had fallen asleep without realising, she fumbled for her phone, shit, it was gone midnight. Niamh lay beside her, still unclothed. Siobhan took a moment to admire her body, it was so young, flawless. She wished she had appreciated the beauty of her own body when she was younger, not that it had ever looked as good as Niamh's, she'd always been what her mother called "Sturdy." She watched Niamh for a few moments longer, her breasts rising and falling with her breathing, she then quietly slipped out of the bed and began to dress. Niamh stirred in the bed.

"I have to go, I'm sorry"

"When will I next see you?"

"It's the funeral on Friday, I'll call you after that"

"OK" Niamh sat up sleepily and kissed Siobhan. Siobhan inhaled deeply, smelling Niamh's hair and perfume, she kissed her back and then gathered up her belongings.

It was too late to catch the train home so she ordered an Uber and waited outside for "Mohammed in a Toyota Avensis". She prayed when he arrived that he wouldn't be in the mood for conversation, she just needed to sit in silence for a while, think about what had happened that night and work out where the hell she went from there.

Chapter thirteen

The alarm sounded at 7am, she wasn't in court but she still had to get the kids up and make sure they got to school on time. She winced as she sat up, she hadn't drunk that much but the memory of the night flooded her. She wasn't sure she could do this, live a lie, but at the same time she wasn't ready to give it up either.

She pulled her dressing gown on and shoved her feet into well worn slippers. Filling the kettle as she yawned she couldn't quite believe what had happened. The routine of her daily life felt so normal, mundane, compared with the excitement of Niamh, it was as if she was living someone else's life. Her thoughts were interrupted as Dan put his arms around her waist.

"You alright love, didn't hear you come in?"

"Yeah, got chatting over the wine, you know how it is"

"Did you manage to get your Mom's thing written?"

"Most of it, I'm going to work on some more of it today. You got work?"

"Yeah, just a quick job, I'll hopefully be home for lunch," Dan looked at her carefully "You look tired, you OK?"

"Well, my Mom just died and I'm trying to write something meaningful in her memory, so no, not really" Dan looked offended. "Sorry, didn't mean it to sound a stupid question, just trying to see if you're alright"

Siobhan felt guilty, he looked like a wounded child, she hadn't meant to snap at him.

"I know, just dealing with a lot at the moment. Let me get the kids sorted, a day at home by myself will do me good"

By 8.50am the house was silent and Siobhan sank into the sofa gratefully. She knew she had to finish writing but her mind was all over the place. Why had Niamh reacted so strongly, what more did she want from her? She kept replaying the events of the evening and felt a small tug of warning that she couldn't quite dismiss.

She set the laptop up and began to write. Every so often she would have to pause as the emotion became too much for her and she was unable to see through the tears but she finally had something she felt did her mother's life justice.

The day of the funeral arrived, a typical January day, dark, overcast, the skies heavy with threatened rain. As Siobhan dressed she couldn't help but think that at least her work wardrobe of black suits gave her plenty of options to choose from.

The car was arriving at 10.30am so she had time to fix her hair and apply her make up. She had tried to eat breakfast but she couldn't stomach anything. She noticed that Emily hadn't eaten either and, not for the first time since her mother died, she worried about whether her daughter was coping. Ben had seemed more robust, he had always been a pragmatic child and this to him was part of the order of things. Then again, boys weren't renowned for talking about their feelings and there was always the possibility that he was bottling it all up inside. She tried to be cheery with the children "How are we guys?"

"OK Mom" came Ben's response, whilst Emily just stared morosely at her phone. She had considered asking them whether they wanted to say anything, or play a part in the funeral mass, but at 9 and 12 they were just that bit too young.

Dan was standing before the mirror in the bedroom, struggling with this tie. He only had one suit, and it made an appearance at weddings and funerals. She noticed the buttons were straining at the waist and the suit jacket wouldn't quite meet.

"Need a hand?"

Dan smiled gratefully and Siobhan expertly tied his tie. He always looked handsome in a suit, and despite the mood she couldn't help but kiss him. Part of her wished he had a more professional job, that he would wear a suit more often, but he loved being an electrician and you couldn't exactly rewire a house in a three piece.

"You ok love?"

"Not really, but I just want to get through it"

"I know" he put his arms around her and once again she felt that safety that only his hugs could bring. She felt herself begin to cry again.

"Now my mascara is running! You know what, I don't think I'll wear any, it's only going to make me look a mess"

She fixed her makeup again and then went downstairs to make sure that Ben's school shoes were clean. He was going to wear his school trousers and shirt, then a tank top she had found lurking in the back of his wardrobe, Emily had a black skirt and top on. She looked older suddenly and Siobhan found herself worrying about where their childhoods were going.

The doorbell rang and she checked herself over once more in the mirror, straightened her shoulders, and then opened it to the funeral director.

"Mrs Smith? I'm so sorry for your loss"

She doubted he was, he hadn't known her mother, didn't know the gaping hole her death had left in Siobhan's life, but she knew he had to say it and she resisted the urge to make a sarcastic comment in response.

"Thank you. Just give me a moment please and I'll get everyone out"

Coats found, shoes tied the family trooped out of the front door. Siobhan had checked her handbag, making sure she had plenty of tissues, and her speech. The flowers were already in the car and Siobhan gulped as she saw the white carnations laid out on the coffin. She wasn't ready for this, she couldn't go through with this, the idea of her mother being buried in the ground under 6 foot of muddy earth was almost too much to bear.

"Dan I can't" she looked at him panic stricken, he didn't know what to say but he took her arm and gently guided her towards the car. Ben was excited at being in a limousine, for him this was all one big adventure, whereas Emily stared out of the car window with dark, hollow eyes.

As they set off for the church the rain began. Siobhan noticed people pausing as the funeral procession went past, some older folks even made the sign of the cross and Siobhan silently thanked them.

The car park at church was almost full, and once again Siobhan realised just how many people her mother had touched. The mourners all stood back respectfully as the coffin was unloaded from the car, then without direction, they formed a line behind Siobhan and her family as they all followed the coffin into church. Father Flynn was waiting at the doors to welcome them in, and the procession took their seats.

Siobhan couldn't look Father Flynn in the eye, for fear of losing control of her emotions again. She knew he was talking but the words were just passing through her. She was concentrating all of her efforts on holding it together just long enough to get through the eulogy. When the Priest called upon her she thought her legs might give way as she walked to the altar.

Dan gave her a reassuring smile as she stood at the lectern, she felt her fingers trembling as she unfolded her speech.

"How do you sum up a person's life in just a few words, how do you do it justice? That is what has troubled me for the last few weeks, how do I make sure the world knows about Margaret, Maggie Flaherty, and sit down without worrying there is something I have forgotten. The reality is I don't need to say anything, just looking at so many people who have come to say goodbye tells me that you already know what a wonderful person she was, the good she did in her life. I know from looking at your faces that you will miss her as much as I already do…

As Siobhan settled into her eulogy she looked into the faces of different mourners, saw the tears in their eyes and felt the pain they were suffering. She recognised so many of her mother's friends, and was heartened that they had turned out, despite the unrelenting weather. Their faces turned to smiles when she mentioned the good works her mother had done, they laughed at the memory of her mother jumping up and down in excitement the day she thought she had won the main Bingo prize, only to find out she was wearing her old glasses and had misread some of the numbers.

Siobhan was just coming towards the end of her remarks, she had been looking down at the piece of paper before her and as she looked up she caught sight of Niamh at the back of the church. The unexpectedness of it caused her to stumble and she almost lost her thread, she felt herself go dizzy and had to take a moment to stop the words from swimming before her eyes. She could feel the congregation looking at her, Dan started to move from his seat but before he got to the end of the bench she had recovered herself and was able to finish the eulogy.

She was trembling as she regained her seat, the emotion threatening to overwhelm her and the fear she had felt in her stomach when she caught Niamh's eye. What was she doing here? Had anyone else noticed? As she sat down Emily reached for her hand and Siobhan took it gratefully, Dan leaned over and whispered "well done" into her ear, Siobhan smiled weakly but didn't respond. She took a few deep breaths to try and calm herself down, to anyone watching it would simply seem that she was upset and trying not to cry whereas Siobhan felt an anger rising inside her that she was fighting to control.

Father Flynn had begun to talk, he had known her mother many years, and gave a personal account of her contributions to the church. Siobhan had been to a number of funerals where the Priest simply recited platitudes that, quite frankly, could be adapted to anyone, but in this case it was clear he had held a genuine affection for Margaret Flaherty and the warmth with which he spoke was genuine.

Siobhan had chosen the hymns but she struggled to find her voice and she could only mouth the words to the Great Redeemer. As the final hymn of Abide with me rang out she couldn't hold the tears any longer and she sat in the bench and sobbed. The pall bearers wheeled the coffin down the aisle and Siobhan followed behind, unable to make eye contact with anyone, the grief overwhelming her.

Her mother, ever the pragmatist, had bought a burial plot some years earlier, thus all the pall bearers had to do was wheel the coffin along the path outside the church, and then lift it onto the adjacent grass. There had already been two funerals that year and the mounds of the fresh graves stood proud, leaving Siobhan to feel that at any moment a hand would burst through them.

Father Flynn stood at the graveside as the coffin was lowered to the ground, the final prayers said, and the dirt scattered over the shining mahogany. It was drizzling with rain but the funeral director had done his best to shield the family with large, black umbrellas. They felt threatening somehow and added yet another sombre layer to the already serious proceedings. She stood closest to the grave, her children and Dan beside her, the other mourners a respectful distance back. Siobhan looked up again, her eyes casting around the graveside to see if Niamh was still there, she spotted her, standing thirty or so feet away. Niamh was looking straight at her and Siobhan felt her chest pounding, praying that she would come no closer. As she looked closer she realised that Niamh wasn't standing alone, she was with Sarah and Parmjit from chambers, she felt a wave of relief flood through her, Niamh hadn't come to the funeral to announce their secret, she was just there, with her friends as support. She began to cry again, with relief this time that her secret was still safe. Dan, seeing his wife in tears put his arm around her shoulder, which only made her cry harder. She reached her hand out and pulled Ben and Emily closer, she took a deep breath and tried to compose herself.

Once the Priest had finished silence enveloped the grave, broken only by the quiet sobs of Siobhan and her children. The wake was to take place in the church hall so the mourners began to file up the path. Siobhan couldn't bring herself to leave, she knew that once the earth was filled in then it would be final, her Mom wasn't coming back, this wasn't a dream she was going to wake up from. She felt Dan's hand on her shoulder "Come on love, its freezing out here and you're getting wet. Time to go." Siobhan didn't reply but she allowed herself to be guided up the path, into the warmth of the church hall where several of her mother's friends had already found the tea urn and were warming themselves besides the outdated heaters.

The moment she walked through the door she was surrounded by well wishers, everyone wanted to pay their respects, tell her how loved her mother was. Siobhan was grateful but all she wanted right now was to curl up in bed and not ever wake up.

She was shaken from her reverie when Sarah and Parmjit approached, with Niamh in tow.

"We're so sorry Shiv, is there anything we can do?" Sarah hugged her friend close, and Parmjit soon joined her. Niamh stood a few inches back but Siobhan caught her eye and smiled weakly.

"Thanks for coming guys, it means a lot"

"You'd do the same for us"

Siobhan looked embarrassed, she wasn't sure she would do the same, she hated funerals and the idea of going to the funeral of a friend's mother seemed a commitment too far – not that she would ever admit that to her friends. "Can I get you a drink? There's tea and coffee, but the bar will be open shortly, wouldn't be a proper Irish funeral without a glass or two"

"We'll just have a tea for now, thanks, anyway, we just wanted you to know we were here" Sarah gave her friend's arm a reassuring rub and went off in search of the tea.

The afternoon seemed to pass in a blur of hugs, tea and memories. People from church she usually only saw one Christmas to the next were at pains to come up and talk. In a way it was comforting, and it distracted Siobhan from her own thoughts, there were few tears as everyone was keen to remember happy memories, it was a celebration of her mother's life, and for that Siobhan was grateful.

By 3pm the numbers were starting to dwindle and Siobhan allowed herself to relax. She ordered a large glass of red from the bar and took a large mouthful, feeling her body relax as the wine took effect. Dan came over to her,

"How are you coping love?"

"Better than I thought, just glad it's here, felt like we were waiting an age for the funeral"

As they chatted Siobhan saw Niamh approach.

"Hello Siobhan, I'm very sorry for your loss"

"Thanks Niamh, it was, er, nice of you to come"

Dan interjected, "Are you not going to introduce me?"

"Dan, this is Niamh, she's chamber's pupil this year, Niamh, my husband, Dan"

"Pleased to meet you Mr Flaherty"

"It's Smith actually, I just use Flaherty for work"

"It's alright, I'm used to being reduced to Siobhan's lesser half"

There was an awkward silence, Siobhan wondered how much Dan resented being referred to by her maiden name, as if his family name counted for nothing.

"Can I get you a drink, Niamh?"

"That would be nice, thank you"

"Dan, can you make sure all the food has been put out, I don't want there to be any left over, otherwise we'll be eating colcannon for a month"

Siobhan watched as Dan went off to speak to the caterers, then she turned to Niamh. "What are you doing here?"

Niamh looked shocked, hurt "I'm here for you Siobhan, I thought you'd want your friends and family around you"

"I do, but don't you think we are risking a lot, what if someone suspects!"

"Suspects what, that you've realised at the age of 44 that actually you like sex with women?"

"Keep your voice down, what if someone hears?!"

"Siobhan, calm down, I'm just a friend from chambers who has come to pay their respects. No one suspects anything, well they won't unless you change that guilty looking puppy face of yours. Now, shall we have a drink together?"

Siobhan looked around nervously, she was being paranoid, Niamh was right, no one was going to think anything of her, she was reliable, dependable Siobhan after all.

"You just took me by surprise, seeing you at the church and everything, sorry, I wasn't expecting it."

"It's Ok, come on, let me get you another glass of wine"

"Chambers rules, pupils don't pay remember, I'll get these. Go and find a seat and I'll come over"

As she was at the bar Philomena Dawson came over and Siobhan found herself chatting about her mother's knitting club for a good ten minutes before she could escape and sit with Niamh.

"Here you go"

"Thanks. To your Mother, may she rest in peace"

Siobhan felt the tears prick her eyes and she raised her glass to toast her Mom. "Amen"

She looked around the hall, self consciously, to see who, if anyone, was watching, but no one was paying attention to Siobhan having a conversation with a work colleague.

"How are you coping? I thought your eulogy was lovely"

"Thanks, I'm OK, I think it's going to be tomorrow when it all hits me, the funeral has been a flurry of activity and decisions having to be made – which casket, what flowers. When it all stops that's when it'll be the worst"

"I thought I might hear from you after Tuesday?"

"Sorry, as I said, lot going on"

Niamh reached over and put her hand on Siobhan's, Siobhan leapt back as if she had been electrocuted, she looked round again to see if anyone had noticed.

"Siobhan, if you react like that then people will think something is up"

"I know, I just, I wasn't expecting it. Please, just be careful"

"It's fine, I am giving you a reassuring pat on the hand at your mother's funeral, its completely normal"

Siobhan felt sick, the guilt was building up inside her and the worry that someone would notice was compounding her misery. "Perhaps you should go, we could meet another time maybe?"

"If that would make you happier, then I'll leave."

"I think I'd be more comfortable, yes. But, I would like to see you again"

"OK, when are you free?"

"I'll text you when I'm done here"

Niamh stood to leave, Siobhan got to her feet and gave her an awkward hug, she didn't dare kiss her, even on the cheek, but it felt nice to be holding her again. Siobhan felt her cheeks burning and pulled away.

"I'll see you soon, thanks for coming"

"Bye, sorry for your loss"

Siobhan watched as Niamh gathered her coat and left the hall. She was still staring after her when she felt Ben's hand slip into hers. It had been a while since he had held her hand and she looked down at him.

"Can I have a cuddle Mom?"

"Oh darling, course you can" she swept him up and held him tight. Waiting for the longest day of her life to be over.

Chapter fourteen

Siobhan lay in bed, reflecting on the funeral and the emptiness she now felt. The anger at the unfairness of it all was receding and now she just felt deflated. She also felt tired, the emotion of the past few days taking their toll. She had a weekend now to recharge before starting back at work on Monday. Her friends had tried to persuade her to take some time off, but she knew it would do no good, she would spend the days slumped in front of daytime television, dwelling, rather than moving forward. She just had the weekend to get through before she could lose herself in the murkiness of sexual assaults and drug dealing.

She hadn't been into chambers for a while and dreaded to think what was in her pigeon hole, urgent advices no doubt requested and ignored, vital discs of evidence lying untouched. First, though, she needed tea and breakfast.

Saturday mornings called for bacon and eggs and soon the smell of frying bacon was waking others who until then had been asleep. Siobhan sat at the kitchen table and smiled as Ben and Emily argued over the last piece of toast, they called each other by increasingly daft insults, Ben resorting to Poo brain when he ran out of ideas. She had never had anything like that growing up, she had been a lonely only child and she had been determined that her children would not experience a similar childhood. Just seeing them teasing each other in this way made her grateful once more for her family.

Leaving a list of housework to be done Siobhan pulled on a pair of jeans and a jumper and searched around for her key fob for chambers. She hadn't been in since Christmas and for a while she couldn't even remember where she had put it. Eventually she found it lurking at the bottom of her work handbag, stuck to a discarded tissue.

The journey to chambers was always so much quicker on a Saturday and Siobhan enjoyed listening to the radio on the way in, without the fear of interruption from solicitors calling for advice, or the clerks chasing her for a piece of work.

Pulling up in the car park next to chambers Siobhan checked her phone for messages.

"Hi, how are you today? N x"

Siobhan paused for a moment, unsure how to reply. "Not too bad, thanks. Just popped to chambers to clear pigeon hole x"

She could tell the message had been read but there was no immediate reply so she grabbed her bag and walked up to chambers. There didn't appear to be anyone else around, clearly others had better things to do than work on a Saturday morning.

As she had feared her pigeon hole was overflowing. She pulled everything out, put the pile on one of the common room tables and made herself a cup of tea in the kitchenette. She sighed and began to work her way through the varying instructions and pieces of correspondence. She could have just taken it all home and sorted through it there but by working in chambers she was less likely to get disturbed.

She had been working for about twenty minutes when she heard the door to the common room open. Niamh was standing there. Siobhan felt her heart rate increase.

"What are you doing here?"

"My pupil master asked me to pick up something for him and when you said you were in chambers I thought I might as well kill two birds with one stone, or at least see two birds"

Siobhan winced at the awful joke and then laughed, the tension in the room easing slightly.

"Seriously, I know we didn't get much chance to talk yesterday so I thought it might be a good idea to see you when its quiet. How are you?"

"Ok, just trying to deal with it all. Still can't quite believe it's happened to be honest"

Niamh came further into the common room and once the door had closed behind her she put her arms around Siobhan.

"I wanted to hug you properly yesterday, you looked so lost"

Siobhan couldn't reply, she had a lump in her throat and was struggling to stop herself crying. She hugged Niamh back and the two stood there holding each other. Siobhan buried her head in Niamh's shoulder and allowed herself to cry properly. Niamh held her, and when the sobbing subsided she took Siobhan's face in her hands and kissed her tenderly. Siobhan felt her body respond and she gratefully kissed her back, needing the affection and the touch more than she had known.

They pulled apart and Siobhan sank into her seat, Niamh pulled a chair alongside her.

"Want a fresh cup?"

"Yes please"

Siobhan watched as Niamh made two cups of tea and brought them over, she had even managed to find the tea lady's secret biscuit stash and Siobhan hungrily ate a chocolate digestive.

"It was dangerous of you to come yesterday"

"I didn't think of it as dangerous, I just wanted you to know I was thinking of you"

"Thank you, you realise though that you freaked me out slightly"

"Sorry, that wasn't my intention. You looked so alone, I just wanted to be there for you"

Siobhan smiled wanly and reached out to hold Niamh's hand.

"I'd like to see you again, properly, if that's OK" said Niamh nervously.

"Yeah, I think I'd like that"

"Maybe next weekend, we could go somewhere for a bite to eat near my place?"

"I'll tell Dan I'm meeting some friends"

"You're getting good at this aren't you?"

"At what?"

"The lying"

Siobhan shifted uncomfortably, of course she knew that she was lying to Dan, she knew she was cheating on him, and yet, because it was with a woman it didn't feel like she was 'having an affair' – the air quotes her own. This was just a deep friendship between two women, and if it meant not being completely truthful with Dan, then that was a price she felt she could live with right now. Niamh stirred her from her thoughts

"Sorry if that sounded blunt, I just meant that you seem to be OK in finding excuses for your husband"

"What about Gemma, she's back from her Christmas break now isn't she?"

"Yeah, but I'm sure she's got a work conference next weekend"

"You never told me what she does, you said you met at Bar school but she's obviously not a barrister in Birmingham"

"She couldn't get pupillage so is just working for one of those firms that sends people to cover small claims and infant settlements"

"Does it not cause any resentment between you? The fact you've got pupillage and she hasn't?"

"No, she understands the cut throat nature of it, she keeps applying and at least she's working in the law"

Siobhan realised that she and Niamh had been chatting for almost an hour and she still had paperwork to sort through. "Look, I'd better get on with this, it was lovely to see you though"

"You too"

They hugged once more, and Siobhan couldn't resist kissing Niamh once more. She watched Niamh leave the common room, she couldn't take her eyes off her and once again wondered just exactly what had happened to her over just a few short weeks. She didn't want to analyse it too much but she knew in reality at least some part of the attraction was having someone wanting her, to feel desired was in itself an aphrodisiac. She also recognised that her life was in a rut, homelife was repetitive, work an endless stream of depressing sex cases, what was happening between her and Niamh felt exciting and dangerous, she felt like a teenager again.

She finished off her work, making sure she had everything she needed for her trial and walked back to her car. She didn't even realise that she had a half smile on her face.

Her first week back at work was difficult, she found it hard to concentrate. The case felt trivial compared to what Siobhan had gone through since finding her mother's body, but she tried her best to remain focussed. It didn't help that her client was a deeply unappealing individual who had been found with thousands of images of child pornography on his computer. Naturally he professed all ignorance as to how they had got there, despite the fact he lived alone and his computer was password protected. Siobhan went through the motions with the Prosecution computer expert, looking at evidence of hacking, or someone remotely accessing his computer, piggybacking off his network. It was futile and her client was duly convicted. The Judge decided that he didn't want a pre sentence report and her client had thus been sentenced straight away.

Downstairs in the cells he was shaking as Siobhan explained that he had no appeal points, and how long he would actually serve in prison.

"But my life is over Miss, I never looked at them pictures"

"I'm sorry Mr Anderson, the jury found that they were sure it was you who had downloaded them"

"But I never did"

"I understand that's your case but you've been convicted now and I'm afraid there's little else I can do"

"You never even asked the expert about computer viruses"

Siobhan started to argue but then checked herself, she was sure she had meant to ask the expert, but thinking back she couldn't actually remember asking the questions. She started to panic, her mind had not been focused on the trial, it had had been alternating between thinking about her mother, to thinking about Niamh. Instinctively she defended herself.

"Mr Anderson the fact is those pictures were on your computer, in your house, on a computer that was password protected and that no one else had access to. It's time to accept the verdict and move on"

She wouldn't normally have spoken so bluntly but she was anxious to deflect from her own potential failings. Before her client had time to respond she was banging on the cell door to be let out. "I'll review the evidence and do a formal written advice"

With that she left the cell. She felt sweat trickle down her back as she considered that actually she had missed out an important line of questioning. Perhaps she shouldn't have come back to work, it wasn't fair on clients if her mind wasn't on the job.

Shaken she left the court building and drove home. The first thing she did was pour herself a large glass of red, she sat in the lounge and drank it.

"You ok?" Siobhan hadn't even noticed Dan come in.

"I think I fucked up today. Client was guilty as sin but I think I forgot to ask some important questions"

"Shit. What you gonna do?"

"I'm going to go over my notes and check. But first I'm going to finish this large glass of wine"

"What's for dinner?"

"Dan I haven't even thought about dinner, I've just said I've had a crap day at work. Why can't you sort something out for once?"

"Look, just cos you messed up, don't take it out on me. You know I hate cooking!"

Siobhan didn't reply for a short time, she just closed her eyes and took another swig of wine. "Let's get a takeaway alright?"

"Fine"

"Fine"

Dan didn't storm out but it wasn't exactly a Hollywood fairy tale goodbye. Siobhan rubbed her temples, she did not need this right now. She sat there for a few minutes longer before pulling out her phone and ordering a Chinese.

When it arrived the family sat in silence at the kitchen table, Emily had her phone out and was idly flicking through it, Dan and Siobhan simply sat silently. Ben looked at them in turn, knowing something was going on but not entirely sure what to say. Siobhan knew she should break the silence but she was tired, tired of being the one to make the effort, tired of pretending that everything was fine. Let them sit awkwardly, she thought, somewhat unkindly.

Dan cleared his throat, Siobhan looked up expectantly, but he just picked up a spring roll and stuffed it in his mouth. She hated that about him, shoving food in rather than trying to cut it up, or eat it with more manners. Not for the first time she felt the tug between her home life and the standards expected at the Bar, the idea of someone at a formal dinner eating like that would be heavily frowned upon, indeed mocked. Siobhan often felt that she had one foot in two worlds, and didn't quite belong in either. Niamh would know what she meant, she could offer sophisticated dining, her flat so tastefully designed with beautiful art hanging on the walls. Niamh would probably have some classical music playing in the background, a nice bottle of red breathing on the side, she wouldn't see how many prawns she could fit in her mouth without choking.

"Can I put some music on?"

It was Emily who broke the silence.

"If you want"

Emily turned the Bluetooth speaker in the kitchen on and began to stream one of her playlists. It could have been any one of a dozen American starlets, with the same cutesy lyrics and poppy beat. On balance Siobhan thought she preferred the awkward silence.

"Have you done your homework?" Hardly an original question but it at least forced the children to talk.

"Yeah" came the single word reply from Emily.

"We didn't have any" said Ben, cheerfully.

That conversation exhausted, Siobhan turned back to her food, she wasn't really hungry and she was just moving rice around the plate. She poured herself another glass of red and took her plate to the sink. "I've got some work to do, I'll work in our bedroom so you can watch TV"

She didn't wait for a reply, but gathered up her laptop and wine and went upstairs.

Sitting on her bed she stared at the computer screen. She knew she ought to review her notes from the trial, start the advice, but the cursor flashed angrily before her and she felt unable to type. In the end she picked up her phone. "Want to meet up on Saturday? X"

She stared at the phone, willing a response. In the meantime Word remained open on her lap top, the blank document almost mocking her.

Her phone buzzed "Would love to. Dinner? X"

"Yes please, maybe somewhere near you? X"

"OK, know a great little Nepalese place, will book table for 8 x"

Siobhan smiled, yes the week had been crap but having dinner with Niamh to look forward to made things seem a little less grim.

She didn't even bother going downstairs to say goodnight, she changed into her pyjamas, found an old Agatha Christie novel and turned her bedside light off just after 10.30pm.

The next morning things were still strained between her and Dan. Siobhan didn't bother with breakfast, she picked up a cereal bar and gulped down a mug of tea.

"I've got bits and bobs in Wolves, I'll see you when I get home"

"Alright, have a good day"

"Meant to say, I'm meeting one of my friends tomorrow night, I may stay over rather than paying for a taxi"

"You going out again?"

"Well if the choice is going out with a friend or watching Britain's Got Talent then I think you'll find it's an easy decision"

"What about me?"

"What about you?"

"Maybe I was going to go out"

"Were you?"

"No, but that's not the point. You've been out loads recently."

"Not that much, this is only the second time in a month, it's not like I have any hobbies or anything"

"Just would've been nice if you'd asked before booking it"

"OK, sorry. Look, I've got to go, I'll see you tonight"

"Bye"

They didn't even bother with the charade of a kiss. Siobhan collected her case and set off for Wolverhampton. She just wanted the day to end and for it to be Saturday night. This was what her life had become now, the only enjoyment and excitement to be found in the arms of a younger woman. Siobhan felt shocked at her own behaviour and knew her mother would be furious with her selfishness. At the same time she couldn't stop herself.

Saturday was the typical round of music lessons and play dates. It was 5pm before Siobhan could begin to get ready. She took some time in choosing her underwear. The vast majority of her underwear drawer comprised of Marks and Spencer stalwarts, pants she wore for comfort, that were going a slightly off white colour now due to how often she had washed them. She didn't want those tonight, she rummaged in the hope of finding something vaguely more appealing, something a little less middle aged. In the end she alighted upon a black bra and pants, they didn't match necessarily but they were marginally more attractive than her "Mom knickers". She opened her wardrobe and looked at it despairingly, black suits she had aplenty, white shirts, no problem. Sophisticated evening wear? Less so. She plumped for a satin shirt and her trusty black trousers, noting she had to breathe in to do them up. She also packed a small overnight bag, dithering over what to put in for both wearing in bed and then also the next morning. She hadn't had to think of things like this since her early days of dating Dan, she noticed she felt a little seedy, rather than perhaps as romantic as she had anticipated.

Dan was on the sofa, zoned out in front of the football.

"I'm off now. Remember I'm staying over tonight, save money on a taxi"

"Yeah you said. Who you meeting again?"

"Just the girls from chambers" she deliberately used the plural.

"What time will you be back in the morning, Ben's got a footy match remember?"

She hadn't remembered, and she felt yet another stab of guilt. "Of course I remembered, I'll be back by 9am"

"Have fun" he said it with no real passion, and there was no kiss as she left.

She drove to Niamh's, knowing that she could park the car in one of the side streets, and it meant she didn't have to endure public transport with the all the pissheads out on a Saturday night. She could feel herself trembling slightly as she drew closer to Niamh's flat, the adrenaline was pumping again and Siobhan had to try and slow her breathing to calm herself down. She tried to remember if she had felt like this in the first few weeks she was with Dan, she couldn't, she hoped it was merely the passage of time that had deadened the memory rather than the chance that she had built her entire life on a romantically unfulfilled basis.

Niamh had booked a table but had arranged for Siobhan to come to hers first so that they could walk over together. Siobhan hadn't brought flowers this time, it felt less like a first date in that respect, but she still shuddered at the anticipation of what was to come. She knew that she would be spending the night in another woman's bed, not leaving in a rush of apologies and guilt- she could barely wait.

Niamh looked stunning as she opened the door, she had a halter neck top on that emphasised the fine structure of her neck and shoulders, the centre of it dipping tantalisingly towards her milky breasts. She was wearing a leather skirt that hugged her hips, and stopped just inches short of her knee, tempting but in some way demure. Siobhan didn't even realise that she was licking her lips.

"Come in beautiful"

Siobhan felt a fraud, she wasn't beautiful, she was dowdy, and saggy and the antithesis of this creature standing before her, she asked herself again why Niamh had chosen her. Sensing her hesitation Niamh pulled her inside, closing the door behind her she took Siobhan in her arms and kissed her.

"I see you have an overnight bag with you?"

Siobhan could hear the flirtation in Niamh's voice, and she looked into eyes that shone with mischief.

"I'm hoping you haven't packed any pyjamas"

Siobhan couldn't think of anything witty or sexy to say in return "I packed a toothbrush"

Niamh couldn't help but laugh, she may have been the younger of them by some twenty years but Siobhan was like a nervous school girl.

"Tell you what, let's get some food and a couple of gins inside this, then I'll make sure I can find place for your toothbrush"

Siobhan couldn't help but laugh, she knew how she was coming across and was embarrassed by her own behaviour, but as Niamh took her by the hand she knew there was nowhere else she would rather be.

The restaurant was small, and atmospheric, they found a table near the back. Siobhan had never been to a Nepalese restaurant before so she allowed Niamh to order for both of them. Whilst they waited for their food Siobhan poured the wine.

"Are you going to tell me about your week then?"

"You don't want to know"

"Course I do, it's what friends are for isn't it?"

Siobhan began to explain about the week's trials and her fear that she had made a mistake. She found herself unloading on Niamh, explaining how her mind hadn't been on the job, how she cared less about work at the moment and how she was worried that maybe she just wasn't up to it anymore. As Niamh listened sympathetically Siobhan realised how much she needed this, someone to actually listen to her, to understand what she was going through without having to explain all the acronyms. So many of her friends had married fellow barristers and Siobhan could now understand the attraction. It was also nice to not be talking about the mundanity of homelife, not worrying if they had changed their gas tariff that month or whether the broadband was up for renewal. In short she was escaping what her life had become and it felt so good.

Two courses, a bottle of red and two gins later Siobhan could feel her eyes starting to go slightly fuzzy, a sure sign she had drunk too much. As they walked out of the restaurant Niamh slipped her arm through hers and Siobhan rested her head against Niamh's shoulder, taking comfort from the warmth and friendship it offered.

When they got back to the flat Niamh didn't have to say anything, she just kissed Siobhan and took her through to the bedroom.

Siobhan had never experienced a night like it, she abandoned herself to Niamh completely, she let her teach her what she had never learned before. It was 4am before she closed her eyes and succumbed to sleep.

Chapter fifteen

A distant buzzing roused Siobhan from her deep sleep. At first she couldn't recall where she was, or why she wasn't in bed. As she came to she realised she was naked, she hadn't slept naked in years. The buzzing persisted and Siobhan groggily sat up, she reached for her phone, the buzzing stopping just as she managed to grasp it.

3 Missed calls. Shit. She focused on the time, 10.07am. Shit! 6 text messages. As she held the phone it buzzed again.

WHERE THE FUCK R U

Danny, fuck, fuck, fuck. Siobhan scrabbled to sit up, next to her the naked body of Niamh still slumbering next to her. The realisation dawned upon her, Ben's football game at a local school had been due to kick off at 10am, she had promised to take him and his friend as Emily had a trip to the cinema for a friend's birthday. Panicking, she couldn't decide what to do first, phone Dan or get dressed. She decided phoning Dan wasn't going to help at this stage so she began to search for her clothes. Cringing she retrieved her underwear from a corner of the room where it had been swiftly abandoned last night. Her clothes were in a puddle on the floor. She stuffed them into her overnight bag and pulled out a fresh top and jeans. Niamh still slept on, unaware of the problems building up in Siobhan's life.

Siobhan crept into the bathroom and quickly brushed her teeth and pulled a brush through her hair. She looked like hell but it would have to do. Steeling herself she texted Dan "Overslept, sorry, on way now"

"DON'T BOTHER RUSHING. HAVE TAKEN BEN TO FOOTY, EMILY WITH ME, CRYING"

Oh God, Emily would never forgive her for making her miss the cinema trip, Dan was clearly seething, part of her just wanted to stay here, in the pretend little world she had created for herself, but she knew she had to get back to reality.

She went into Niamh, she stopped for a moment and watched her perfect face as she slept, at rest her mouth opened slightly, her lips so inviting, her body flawless. Siobhan gently brushed her shoulder, feeling the curve of her spine as it disappeared tantalisingly below the covers.

Niamh began to stir.

"I'm sorry, I have to go"

"Mmmm?"

"I overslept, I have to go now, I'll try and call during the week"

Niamh propped herself up on one elbow.

"You ok?"

"No, I'm late for family stuff, I think Dan may suspect something, he's furious. I'm sorry but I really have to go"

"Don't leave, stay for coffee at least"

"Niamh I'm sorry, this is family, I have to"

Niamh looked wounded as Siobhan pulled away, Siobhan couldn't look her in the eye as she pulled her coat on and walked out into the cold air.

On the drive home she racked her brains as to which school the game was at, she tried to work out whether she could make it back, collect Emily and still get her to the cinema. The traffic was light and she was pulling onto the school car park by 10.50am, frantically she jumped out of the car and ran over to where a small group of parents stood huddled in large coats, trying to protect themselves from the freezing weather whilst their boys ran around a muddy football pitch. She scanned the crowd and quickly spotted Dan, standing with his arm around Emily.

"I'm here, I made it"

Dan turned and glowered at her, he said nothing.

"Mom the film started at 10.45am, I've missed it!"

"I'm so, so sorry darling, I didn't set the alarm on my phone and then I overslept!"

"I hate you!"

Siobhan looked desperately at Dan for some support, Emily had never spoken to her that way before, still he remained silent.

"Emily, hate is a really strong word to use, I know you're disappointed, and I'm sorry. Perhaps the adverts are still on, if we go now we might make the beginning of the film"

"It's too late, they'll all have gone in, it would be too embarrassing to walk in now, they'll all laugh"

"Well we could try?"

"I just want to go home"

"Ok, come on"

"Not with you, with Dad"

Siobhan looked helplessly at Dan.

"You stay here and watch Ben, I'll take Emily home"

"Dan, I'm sorry"

"We'll talk at home. I'll see you later"

Putting his arm around Emily's shoulder he stalked back to their car. Siobhan was conscious of other parents who had clearly heard what was going on but were trying desperately to pretend they hadn't noticed. Middle class politeness at its best.

Siobhan felt her eyes welling up, thankfully it was so cold she could put it down to the winter air and hope that no one noticed. Ben was oblivious to it all and was currently charging down the left side of the pitch in a hopeless attempt to get the ball. Siobhan tried to shout words of her encouragement but her heart simply wasn't it.

Once the game was over she bundled Ben and George into her car, dropped George off at his parents and then drove home to face the music.

As she opened the door she could hear music blaring from Emily's bedroom. Dan was in the garage tinkering with his bike.

"Go and have a shower love then I'll do you some lunch"

Ben disappeared upstairs, Siobhan tentatively opened the door to the garage.

"We're home"

Dan looked up, his face clouded with anger.

"About fucking time!"

"Don't swear, the kids are home. I know you're furious, and I'm sorry, but let's try and be grown ups"

"Grown ups don't stay out all fucking night and forget about their kids' parties and football games"

"I know, I said I'm sorry. It won't happen again"

"I don't know what's wrong with you, these last few months you just haven't been here"

"What do you mean, I haven't been anywhere"

"Don't cross examine me, you know what I mean. Late home, going out drinking, coming home at all hours. Yeah you may be here like as in physically here but your mind is elsewhere!"

"I've been through a lot, losing my Mom, you know that!

"This started before that, before Christmas you were out, leaving me and the kids. Tell me, have you met another bloke?"

"No", said Siobhan truthfully, "I promise, I haven't. I think, work was maybe getting to me, you know how busy it is before Christmas and I was travelling then, then losing my Mom I've just been dealing with that by kind of drinking to forget"

"You're not a fucking teenager Siobhan, you're 44 years old, with two kids and husband at home that need you"

"Need me? Really? Or just need someone to cook the dinners and clean up after you!"

She was shouting now, the frustrations of the last few years bubbling to the surface "You don't want a wife, you want a fucking housemaid!"

Dan looked shocked, Siobhan rarely swore in anger and he hadn't expected this reaction. Siobhan noticed that she was trembling.

"Is that how you feel?" his tone was softer, a slight hint of conciliation there.

"Sometimes, yeah, I get up, sort out the kids, go to work, come home, cook, clean, do my work, go to bed and get up and do it all the next day. We barely go out together, I'm a glorified taxi service for the kids and our nights consist of you watching the same crap on tv whilst I work till all hours on some shitty sex offender"

They both stared at each other, Dan had a spanner in his hand and Siobhan noticed he was twirling it nervously.

"I guess we've both been a bit crap haven't we?"

"Yeah, I guess so. Dan I am sorry, it was just a night out and I had a few too many drinks, I'm sorry about Emily's party and about letting you down. I'm not going to win Mom of the year any time soon but I'm doing my best" This wasn't true and she felt guilty even as she said it, but she was also relieved that at least Dan knew how she was feeling now. Perhaps this "thing" with Niamh had just been a reaction to the frustrations of her own life, it had been exciting but it wasn't worth feeling the way she currently felt.

She held out a hand to Dan. He took it and they stood there for a short time. "Shall we go out for Sunday lunch somewhere, as a family?"

"Yeah, that'd be nice, maybe the carvery in Sutton park?"

"Yeah. I'm sorry Dan, I think we've both been taking each other for granted. No more OK?"

"Ok. Let me get out of these oily clothes and we'll get some grub. You'd better work it out with Emily though too, she's pretty pissed"

"I know. I'll go and see her now"

Siobhan breathed a sigh of relief as she left the garage, Danny had clearly suspected something was going on, thankfully he was so naïve it had never occurred to him that the other man was in fact another woman. Now she just had Emily to deal with. Siobhan crept up the stairs and knocked on Emily's door, the music was still blasting. She knocked again, slightly louder, then walked into the room.

Emily's head was buried in her phone, her fingers furiously texting.

"Hey"

Emily didn't look up. Siobhan stood there, slightly embarrassed. "Emily" Emily paused and looked at her mother, her eyes flashing with anger.

"What?"

"Please don't use that tone with me. I know you're angry but we can still speak civilly to one another"

Emily didn't answer, Siobhan wasn't sure how to start the conversation. "Emily, I'm sorry, I know I let you down. It won't happen again, I promise. I was thinking maybe you and I could go into Sutton next weekend and perhaps go shopping and maybe lunch together?"

Still nothing but at least Emily hadn't shouted at her, or returned to her phone.

"I know this party meant a lot to you, and it's totally my fault you missed it. I get that you are angry and I am really, really sorry"

"I really wanted to go to that party Mom, all my friends were there, and at school tomorrow they'll all be talking about how good the film was"

"I know, I understand and if I could turn back the clock and not be late you know I would do, but I can't, I can only say I'm sorry and keep saying sorry." She stood there, not quite sure what to say next. "Well, ok then, we're going to go out for Sunday lunch in a bit so you'd better get ready"

She didn't expect a reply, she closed the door quietly and went into her bedroom. Her phone was in her pocket and she took it out. She held it in her hand and stared at it for a while. Eventually she started to type

"Sorry had to dash, I was late for family event..." The cursor flashed, Siobhan was trying to compose a message that ended all this, the subterfuge, the guilt, she just wasn't cut out for it. She started to type again "I don't think it's a good idea to keep doing this, can we talk over coffee next week? X"

She pressed send and put her phone away. She needed a shower, something to wash away the night, the grubbiness she felt in every sense. She turned the hot water on and stood beneath the shower, letting the hot water wash over her. She felt tired, tired of the hiding and the secrecy, tired of what she had done. She resolved that it was over, no matter the temptation.

Dressed, Siobhan went downstairs, Dan had changed into a smart shirt and had even put some gel in his hair in an effort to tame it.

"You look handsome"

"Thanks, you look Ok yourself"

"Ever the charmer. Are the kids ready?"

"I'll go check"

20 minutes later they were at the carvery, enjoying the smell of the roast meat selection. Dan had a pint, Siobhan had a glass of red, and for the first time in weeks she properly relaxed. There was a short wait for a table to become free, Siobhan felt her phone buzz in her handbag. She knew who it was likely to be and she didn't want to risk getting her phone out in front of the family so she ignored the sound and hoped no one else would notice. After a few minutes she excused herself to go to the toilet, there she was able to check her phone in peace.

"What happened? Please don't leave me. I need you x"

It was worse than Siobhan had feared. Her head began to swim and she tried to think clearly. She wanted to send a message that conveyed how much she had enjoyed what had happened, but that it couldn't go on, but she knew there was so much at stake that one wrong word could ruin everything. She sat in the cubicle and felt like crying, how could it have come to this, it was her own fault and she had to sort this mess out now.

"Dan nearly guessed. My fault, not yours. Please can we talk about this in person, not over text? X"

She didn't dare wait for a reply so flushed the toilet and hurried back to her family. They were just being shown to a table by the waitress and she followed anxiously, trying not let them see her panic.

Considering the circumstances the meal could be deemed a success. Emily had thawed and was at least speaking to her mother, Ben was happy enough as he'd played football, won, and now had several Yorkshire puddings on his plate – it didn't take much to make a 9 year old happy. Dan seemed relieved to have got matters off his chest earlier and he was busily telling them about the state of some of the wiring he had found in a house the previous week.

Siobhan was quiet, but she enjoyed the buzz and chatter of her family around her. She just sat there, soaking it all in. It was nearly 3pm by the time they had finished, Siobhan had managed a sticky toffee pudding and now felt full and lethargic as they made their way back to the car.

"Fancy putting on a film when we get in?"

"Lego movie!" Shouted Ben enthusiastically.

"Perhaps something we could all enjoy, let's watch one of the classics, like Annie or Oliver!"

Emily rolled her eyes "Mom, we're not 5!"

"Ok, you suggest one"

They bickered happily throughout the car journey home and finally agreed on Back to the Future.

It was still bitterly cold outside so Dan put the fire on, he even made hot chocolate with whipped cream. The four of them curled up on the sofas, dimmed the lights, and enjoyed the film. Siobhan couldn't remember the last time they had done something like this as a family, she realised just how much she had missed it, the reality was the kids simply didn't need her as much anymore, they had been all been living increasingly disparate lives and it had taken the shock of the morning's events to make her realised what she had almost thrown away. She knew she still had work to prepare for tomorrow, but at the moment that could wait, it felt more important right now to just sit with her family. She felt her eyes begin to close as the John Williams theme tune blared out of the television. She knew that next week she had some difficult conversations ahead, she knew her phone was buzzing, with unanswered messages, but for now she wanted to put that aside and enjoy the Sunday. She was happy.

Chapter sixteen

Siobhan's eyes felt gritty when she woke up, she had worked late to finish prepping the week's trial, a decision she was regretting now. She noticed that as she got ready for work she felt lighter somehow, the burden of the secret she had been carrying these last few months had been lifted from her and was looking forward to the prospect of getting her teeth into the next case.

She ruffled Ben's hair as he sat eating his Weetabix. "Mo-oo-m"

"Sorry love, couldn't resist. You got everything you need for school?"

"Yeah, is my PE kit clean?"

"All washed, in the bag by the front door"

"Thanks"

"Dad is dropping you in, I'm in Stafford today so I'll see you tonight"

"K, see you later"

She kissed the top of his head, even though he tried to pull away. Dan was in the bathroom, shaving, Siobhan popped her head around the door. "I'm off now love, I'll see you tonight"

"Alright love. Listen, do you want me to try and cook dinner tonight?"

Siobhan was so surprised she didn't answer for a moment. "Wow, I mean, do you want to?"

"Well when you said yesterday that I never did anything it made me think a bit, and yeah I suppose you do do all the cooking and stuff, so I thought I could maybe help a bit"

"OK, I've just left some chicken breasts in the fridge to defrost, I was going to do them with mini roasties, veg and chorizo. It's pretty simple, all you have to do is chop the veg, and whack it all in together with one of the packet sauces."

"Sounds simple enough. I'll aim for dinner at 6.30"

"Fine by me. Have a good day, see you later"

Siobhan was still in a slight state of shock as she pulled off the drive, Dan had never shown any inclination to cook, he must have been really hurt on Sunday if this is what it had led to.

The journey to court was uneventful, the usual Monday morning traffic and queues into Stafford. Siobhan was determined to be focussed on her case this week, she couldn't afford any more slip ups like the last one.

She signed in for her case in the robing room, it was a sexual assault, allegation of a doorman taking advantage of customer trying to get into the nightclub he was working at. Siobhan smiled at the name of the nightclub, it had been a good source of income for her over the years, a mix of violence, drug offences and the odd sexual assault. She was amazed it still had its licence but as long as it kept her in work she wasn't going to complain.

She went off to find her prosecutor, it was Mary Aston, she was employed by the CPS directly which had its pros and cons. On the one hand it meant she had no financial interest in cracking a case, she would be paid the same regardless of whether it was a trial or not, on the other if there was a prospect of doing a deal at least she was authorised to make a decision without having to leap through various hoops and check with various line managers.

"Morning Mary, how's tricks, long time no see?"

"Hello stranger. Haven't seen you in a while, are we against each other today?"

"Yep, case of Barnett, touchy feely doorman?"

"Oh him! I need to check but I'm pretty sure we've had a message to say our witness doesn't want to come to court"

Siobhan tried not to get her hopes up, if the witness was refusing to come to court the CPS had no other evidence, it would mean they would have to drop the case against her client – a great result and an early finish, on the other hand the CPS could apply for a witness summons, or send Police round to the witness's house to try and persuade her to come – which would mean a day of hanging around, drinking machine coffee and maybe not getting the trial up and running. She tried her best to keep her voice neutral "So, what's the witness saying?"

"Not sure yet, she left a couple of messages last week but nobody in the office got back to her. Go and grab a coffee and I'll try and find out what's happening"

Siobhan checked her watch, the client had been told to be here for 10am and it was only just 9.30am, she had time to wander into Stafford and get herself a decent coffee from the local

Starbucks. Feeling reckless she wandered out of the building and into the town centre. It was cold, but a clear blue sky, the route into town took Siobhan through the churchyard and down some cobbled streets, the old sweet shop almost tempted her but she managed to resist. In a blatant attempt at bribery she bought herself a latte, and a cappuccino for Mary.

Going back through security she had to carry out the ridiculous sip test, where she was made to take a drink out of each cup to prove she wasn't trying to smuggle poison or acid into the building. Bill, the old security guard, winked at her when she just put her lips to the cup

"Go on love, we know its coffee, just put on a show of drinking it in case the powers that be are watching"

Siobhan loved Bill, he had a wicked sense of humour and minimal respect for his employers. She took the coffee straight round to the CPS room. Mary was just finishing a phone call.

"So, turns out the witness called the Police twice last week to say she wasn't coming to court. She says she was drunk and can't really remember what happened, but she doesn't want to come to court and go through it all"

"What are you going to do? Summons her?

"Nope, she's made her mind up, and if she says she was drunk and can't remember it undermines our case somewhat, especially as your chap was sober and is of good character. We're going to drop it, I've already let the usher know"

"Cheers, Mary, oh, I got you a coffee – obviously a flagrant attempt to get you to drop the case, looks like I needn't have bothered."

Mary grinned, "I'll take it anyway thanks. I'll get my kit on and we can get the case on sooner rather than later."

"Fab, I'll find my client and give him the good news"

Siobhan walked up the stairs to the landing where all of the parties waiting for their cases to be heard congregated. Although she had never met her client before it didn't take her long to spot him, 6ft 5, 20 stone, shaven head. "Mr Barnett?"

"Uh, yeah?"

"Hello, Siobhan Flaherty, your Barrister"

"Oh right"

"Let's find a conference room and I'll explain what's happening"

Siobhan found a small conference room to the side of court three, it had the usual detritus of discarded coffee cups, and used tissues and Siobhan almost wiped the seat before sitting down.

"So, good news, the witness in your case, the one who said you had touched her when she was going into the club, has refused to come to court. It means the prosecution are going to drop the case and you'll be found not guilty. The case will be finished today"

Her client looked at her open mouthed, he was trying to process what he had just been told. Siobhan sometimes forgot the pressure defendants were under, this offence had taken place nearly 14 months previously, the client had been suspended from work all that time, and now, just like that, he was told it was all over and he could get back to work, no wonder it took a little time to take in.

"So, like, that's it?"

"Yep. We'll go into court, the Prosecutor will tell the Judge what I've just told you, and then he'll formally enter a not guilty verdict"

"That's brilliant! I mean, thank you so much"

To her embarrassment he actually began to cry. So much for stereotypes, she thought as she watched the giant of a man before her sob.

"I need to phone my wife, she's pregnant and I didn't want her to come to court"

Days like this made the job worthwhile, the truth was Siobhan had done nothing to facilitate this outcome but now a man who had never been in trouble with the Police before was going to be able to go home to his wife and tell her it was all over, no conviction, he could go back to work and provide for his unborn child. She was still smiling to herself when Mr Barnett stood up and grabbed her in a bear hug.

"Thank you so much!"

"You're welcome" said Siobhan as she fought to extricate herself from his grip.

She watched him walk out of the conference room, still clearly stunned, and then he began to make his phone calls, and spread the good news.

Siobhan was done in court by 10.45am. She watched her client leave the building, him still in stunned disbelief, her quietly satisfied. She now had to go into chambers, check her pigeon hole and find out what tomorrow held as she had expected this trial to run for the next few days. Oh well, an early bath and a day out of court weren't exactly the worst things in the world. With any luck she might be able to get home early and have the place to herself for a few hours.

She pulled out of the car park happily, the rush hour traffic was gone and the journey into Birmingham was easy, she even found herself singing along to the radio.

Chambers was busy, not everyone had been fortunate enough to have such a short day, junior clerks were running around with large piles of post and briefs, the phone never stopped ringing at reception. Siobhan walked up to the pigeon hole room, collected the contents and then wandered off to the common room to go through it all.

She stopped in her tracks after she had opened the door, Niamh was working at the large communal table. She hadn't readied herself for this, and didn't want to have any discussion about what had happened in a busy chambers that seemed to have ears everywhere. She paused, she was going to turn around and work elsewhere but before she could close the door Niamh looked up.

"Hi"

"Hello" even saying that sounded awkward in Siobhan's mind.

"It's great to see you"

"Nice to see you too. How come you're not in court?"

"Oh, John's trial cracked so he sent me back over here to write a case summary on one of his other cases. What about you?"

"Cracked, just thought I'd come and clear my pigeon hole"

"Oh. You never replied to me you know"

"Niamh, we can't talk about this here, there are too many people" Siobhan looked around nervously, wondering who may be in the corridor outside, listening in.

"Please, I need to see you"

"I'm right here!"

"You know what I mean"

"Niamh, we can't do this now" Siobhan was hissing through gritted teeth, she could feel her heart racing, but not out of excitement, or anticipation, this time only fear as to what Niamh may do or say next. She noticed Niamh had begun to well up, that was the last thing she needed, someone to walk in and see the Pupil in tears. "Look, its nearly lunch time, why don't we go and grab a bite to eat, somewhere a bit quieter, and we can try and talk about this"

Niamh bit her lip, the tears brimmed at the edge of her eyelids, but thankfully didn't spill over. Siobhan realised she was holding her breath, she tried to breathe out calmly, not betraying the panic that was swelling inside her. How could she have been so stupid? She was a tenant, Niamh was a Pupil, she could end up in front of the Bar Standards Board, facing being disbarred for taking advantage of her. Oh God, if she was disbarred, what would she do? She wasn't qualified to do anything else, she didn't want to do anything else. Dan would find out. Oh God!

"Niamh?"

"OK, let me just message John so he knows where I am"

Siobhan waited anxiously as Niamh typed out her message. She was trying to think about where they could go, this part of town was always teaming with lawyers, especially at lunchtime and she was bound to be spotted. In the end she settled upon the Bacchus Bar, it was underground, meaning there was no chance of any passing barrister spotting them through the window, it was also the other side of town from chambers, so unlikely that anyone would be lunching there.

"I know a great little bar that does light bites for lunch, I think you'll like it" She wondered if Niamh noticed the forced levity in her voice.

They walked across Colmore Square in silence, the other workers hurried past, it wasn't the weather to be dawdling outside. As they walked past House of Fraser Niamh put her hand out as if to take Siobhan's in hers, Siobhan recoiled back, as if she'd been bitten. She saw tears brim in Niamh's eyes again.

As she had hoped Bacchus was quiet, not many people treated themselves to lunch on a Monday. They found a corner table, no one could sit behind them and Siobhan could survey the bar so on the off chance anyone did walk in Siobhan would at least be able to see them before they could see her.

She picked up the menu and made a great play of studying it, trying to work out what she was going to say. A bored waitress came over. "Can I get you ladies anything?"

"Just a diet coke for me thanks"

"Mineral water thank you" Niamh's voice was barely a whisper.

Siobhan paused until the waitress was out of earshot. "Niamh, thank you for coming to lunch. I said we needed to talk, I guess I just wasn't expecting it to be so soon"

Niamh interrupted her "How could you leave me like that, not knowing, what have I done wrong?"

"It's not you, it's me" Even as the words escaped her mouth Siobhan grimaced. "Sorry, didn't mean to sounds like a fucking cliché". Niamh at least had the courtesy to raise a half smile.

"Let me try again. I overslept on Sunday and when I got back Dan was furious, he started questioning where I'd been, what I'd been doing. He'd noticed that I seemed distracted, and also that I had been going out a bit more. He straight out asked me if I was seeing another man. I was able to look him in the eye and say I wasn't, but you and I both know I was only giving him half the picture, anyway, I let Emily down as she missed a party and I just realised that I can't do this, I have too much to risk. And it's not just my family, you're a Pupil, I'm a Senior member of chambers, what I'm doing is in breach of the Code of Conduct and I could be risking my career as well. So, I'm sorry, I've really enjoyed what we've had, its awakened something in me that I never knew I had, but it's just too risky and I can't keep doing this to you or my family."

She paused and looked anxiously at Niamh. The words had all come tumbling out and she wasn't sure they had made sense, but she was relieved to have said them.

"So that's it then?" Niamh had an accusing tone in her voice.

"Well, yeah"

"So, you get to decide what's best for us. No thought for my feelings, or what I want?"

"What do you mean 'us'? We're not a couple Niamh, I don't know what we'd call it, but we both knew when this started we were in relationships. Surely you realise that?"

Niamh didn't even try to answer the question "You decide it's over, so it's over, how is that fair?!" Her voice was rising and Siobhan looked around, anxiously, to see if anyone was looking at them.

"Niamh, lower your voice"

"Don't tell me what to do, like you own me or something! You're not my mother!"

"I just mean, look, this is private, between us, ok, I don't want random members of the public listening to our conversations. I hoped we could talk about this like adults"

"Now you're patronising me! How dare you!" Niamh stood up as if to go, Siobhan couldn't let her storm out like this, she had no way of knowing who she might bump into and talk to.

"Niamh please! I'm sorry, I don't know how to say this without upsetting you, but surely you realise that I have got a husband and children, and if they ever find out about this it will destroy them"

"So you're ashamed of being gay now are you?"

"For fucks sake! Firstly, I am not fucking gay, secondly you know that's not what I meant, just the fact I've had an affair could shatter my marriage, and the kids will have to deal with divorcing parents"

"I think you're scared, scared of admitting who you really are Siobhan. I was in bed with you, I saw and felt your body react to mind, don't tell me you're not gay"

"Oh God, this isn't some political thing, I'm not trying to make a point, this is about my marriage, my kids, even my bloody career!"

"You can't do this to me Siobhan, you can't leave me"

"But you're in a relationship too, how would Gemma feel if she found out, you're risking that surely"

"Never mind about that, this is about you and me, and what we have"

"We haven't got anything! This was a few weeks of madness, maybe I'm having a midlife crisis, I don't know OK, but it has to stop."

Niamh began to properly cry at that point, Siobhan could feel her ears and cheeks going red as she looked around, hoping that nobody had noticed the scene unfolding before them.

Siobhan didn't know how to make this any better, this wasn't what she had planned to say or how she thought the conversation would pan out. Her mind was spinning and she was desperately trying to work out how to rescue the situation.

She tried a new tactic "Niamh, you are amazing, when I was with you I felt, I don't know, alive, or just awakened, and it was brilliant, but I'm a grown woman, with responsibilities, and I can't just think of myself and what I want, I have to think of others"

Niamh looked at her and Siobhan could see the pain in those beautiful brown eyes, but at least she had stopped sobbing and appeared to be listening to what she was saying.

"If it was just you and me that I had to think about then things would be different, but it's not, we are both in relationships, I have a husband and two children who would be torn apart from this. Also, don't forget, I am a senior member of chambers, I don't want to put you in a position where you feel like you can't say no to me, it's an abuse of power and that's not fair on you"

Niamh took a hitching breath as Siobhan's words sank in.

"So if you weren't married then you and I might have a future?"

That wasn't what Siobhan had been trying to say but at this point she was so desperate to avoid any further outbursts that she found herself agreeing. "Of course, Niamh, like I said, this isn't just about you and me, if it was then I could be selfish, but we both have others to think of."

This seemed to mollify Niamh, and she visibly calmed. "So, this isn't the end forever?"

"Erm, well, we can't be together now and that's what we have to think about isn't it?"

"OK, I just don't think I could take you not being in my life forever"

"Well that's not going to happen, we're still going to be in chambers together and we'll see each other at events, socially, so it's not like we won't ever see each other."

"Do you promise?'

Siobhan wasn't entirely sure what she was now promising, all she knew was she wanted to get out of this bar, into the fresh air, and away from this spiralling nightmare. "Of course Niamh"

Niamh finally smiled and Siobhan felt a wave of relief wash over her. "Look, we haven't eaten anything yet, do you want to grab a bite here?"

Niamh nodded gratefully. "Well I can recommend the steak baguette"

"Oh no, far too fatty"

Siobhan had forgotten about Niamh's health obsessed diet.

"How about the mussels? Or they do a mean Caesar salad?"

Niamh nodded and Siobhan called the waitress over, the sooner they could eat the sooner she could get out of here. "Just two Caesar salads please"

They waited in an awkward silence for the food to arrive, Siobhan looked around to see who else was in the bar, just a couple of businessmen in the far corner who appeared lost in their own conversation. As Siobhan was looking over to them she felt Niamh's hand on her thigh, instinctively she flinched and pushed it away.

"Niamh, no, we can't!" It was if she hadn't been listening to a word that had been said over the past twenty minutes. Her mind was racing, how the hell could she get out of this situation? Thankfully the food arrived and Siobhan busied herself eating the salad, she was conscious of Niamh watching her eat and her throat felt dry and she tried to swallow the chicken. She cast about for something to talk about that wasn't them and their relationship.

"Any interesting cases you've seen recently?" It sounded pathetic as it came out but anything was better than making Niamh cry again.

"Not really"

That was the end of that conversation. Siobhan could almost hear the minutes ticking by. "How's your salad?"

"Fine"

She gave up, she finished her meal as fast as possible then signalled for the waitress to come over. "I'll get this"

"You can't buy my love Siobhan"

"I'm not, that's not what, Jeez, I'm just paying for a salad!" Siobhan felt flustered again and looked carefully at Niamh to see whether she was going to cause another scene. "Pupils don't pay for lunch, you know that. Come on, lets walk back to chambers so you can get on that with that case summary"

Niamh didn't reach for her hand as they left and Siobhan felt a glimmer of hope, perhaps she had taken what she had said on board, perhaps this was the end of it all and life could get back to its normal, mundane routine. How she'd missed mundanity, she must have been made to risk it all for the sake of a cheap thrill. She felt guilty as she remembered how she had acted, her emotions had taken over and so many people were nearly hurt.

"Look, tonight, when you get in, cook you and Gemma a nice meal, open a bottle of red and forget about me. Enjoy what you have in front of you Niamh."

Niamh didn't reply. They had reached chambers. The Receptionist looked up as they walked through the front door together. Siobhan smiled in acknowledgement then took Niamh into one of the conference rooms. She hugged her "I'm sorry Niamh, I never meant to hurt you."

"It's too late for that" replied Niamh bitterly.

"I'm going now, please, let's stay friends?"

Niamh just stared at her. Siobhan left the room without further words. Her heart raced as she drove home.

Chapter seventeen

Siobhan woke with a start, she took a moment to come to and then realised she had been having a bad dream. Calming down she rolled over and saw Dan lying asleep next to her. He was breathing rhythmically and as she watched his chest rise and fall she felt herself began to calm down.

Her mind flicked back to last night, she had been jumpy all the way home, Niamh's reaction had frightened her and she wasn't sure what she was going to do or say now, she just had to hope that Niamh had as much to lose as she did and would therefore keep their secret. Dan had been too knackered from work to notice Siobhan's mood but Emily had picked up on something. She had even given her mother a cuddle before bed, which, whilst appreciated, had made Siobhan realise that her behaviour was being noticed. She resolved to try and act normally, the affair was over, they both had to move on.

It was just after 6am, she didn't have to be up just yet but it wasn't worth going back to sleep so Siobhan padded downstairs and put the kettle on. The clerks had given her another trial, but it was only in Wolverhampton so she would get chance to take Ben to school before she had to set off.

With the tea cooling in her mug Siobhan sat in the silence of the lounge, she kept replaying the conversation with Niamh and wondering whether she could have handled it differently, she was hopeless at confrontation, put her in a courtroom and she could argue with the best of them, but in a personal setting she shied away from conflict and became tongue tied. She wanted to just forget about everything but she had to drag herself to court and feign enthusiasm for a trial about a fight in Bilston.

Once the children were up the house was the usual hive of activity, Ben seemed to be taking an age to finish his breakfast and Siobhan was becoming impatient.

"Which job are you on today love?"

"Gotta finish the rewire off for that bloke in Erdington, should be home by 5"

"OK, I'm in Wolves, there's a chance my trial might crack but even if it's a runner I'll be home for 5.30pm at the latest. I've got some sausages out of the freezer so I'll just do something with them."

"Sound, have a good day". He actually gave her a proper kiss goodbye and Siobhan enjoyed the feeling of his stubbly chin against her smooth skin, she had missed that physical contact with him and she resolved to make more of an effort with her marriage.

Finally Ben was ready and Siobhan was able to usher him out of the door and then focus her mind on the upcoming trial.

Her client was seen on CCTV squaring up to three other men outside The White Rabbit, he had ripped his top off whilst one of the others had picked up a bottle. Thereafter the CCTV became a little blurry, suffice to say the Police had arrived and arrested all of those at the scene. Her client had a wound to his head, no doubt caused by a bottle launched as a missile, he was claiming self defence, as were all of the others who had been charged. The Crown had charged violent disorder, which Siobhan thought was a bit over the top for what was a standard Saturday night in Bilston.

She got to court and logged on to see who she was co-defending with, the case had affray written all over it and if she could get the other defence teams to agree she could be out of here by lunchtime. Great, all sensible people. She looked around but couldn't see them in the robing room, the obvious place to check next would be the advocate's dining room. Bingo, there they were, enjoying a cooked breakfast at one of the few remaining open canteens. She ordered some toast and coffee and joined them.

"Morning boys"

"Hello Shiv, are you in this pile of crap too?" It was Blake Harrison, one of the more blunt speaking members of the Bar.

"Yep, I'm shirtless guy – covered in blood by the end"

"Oh, I'm bottle guy, apparently he picked it up because you were threatening to rip his fucking head off"

Siobhan sighed, a jury would love this. "How about you Balbir, who have you got?"

Balbir was a young, enthusiastic Barrister who was employed in house with one of the local solicitor's firms.

"My chap is the one who can be seen kicking someone on the floor just before the Police pile in"

"Well, sounds like we've all got really solid defences then! Has anyone offered affray?"

"Trouble is my chap's employer has said if he goes down then he won't keep his job open for him."

"What about a Goodyear" This was a mechanism whereby the Judge could be asked to indicate what sentence he might give if a defendant were to plead guilty.

"Could work, especially as we've got Thomo" Judge Thompson was renowned for being one of the softest judges on circuit, and if the Prosecution could be persuaded to accept an affray then he was their best shot at keeping the defendants out of custody.

"Let's go and find Blair and see if he'll take affray"

Edward Blair was in the robing room and when the four barristers approached him en masse he held his hands up. "I know what you're going to say, you're going to ask me to take an affray aren't you?"

"Oh come on Eddie, you know the Crown only charge violent disorder so that the punters will get frightened and plead to an affray"

"The lawyer has said No, it's a violent disorder"

"But it's a poxy fight in Bilston, who cares?"

"The Police are fed up of dealing with these type of fights every weekend, they want to set an example"

"But the only people they hurt were each other"

"Look, if you can get the Judge to give an indication I might be able to go back to the lawyer and get him to change his mind"

Siobhan nodded to at the others, this was their best shot. They got a message to the usher that if the Judge gave the nod they might be able to sort the trial, the usher would understand the code.

Twenty minutes later Thompson had called them all into court.

"Now, Mr Blair, I've seen the CCTV in this case, unpleasant as it is it seems to me all of the men who were caught up in it are in the dock, it looks like the type of cases to me whereby a few hours serving the community might be the way forward. Violent disorder seems a bit over the top though, that sort of charge belongs to football matches when the hooligans frighten the decent football loving public. Wouldn't affray be more appropriate?"

Blair took the hint, went back to the lawyer and by 12.15pm all of the defendants had pleaded guilty to affray and been sentenced to a community order with 200 hours of unpaid work. They would have to pay the costs but they wouldn't go to prison and they walked out of court together, no doubt headed to the nearest pub.

"Good result Shiv, fancy some lunch?"

"Thanks Balbir, but I'm going to pop home, got some prep I need to get on top of"

This was a lie but Siobhan was so drained by the past few days that she just wanted to have a few hours to herself.

As she pulled onto the drive she noticed that there was something leaning against the front door, she couldn't tell what it was at first but as she got closer she realised it was a bunch of flowers. She smiled, Dan rarely bought her flowers so this was an unexpected treat. She bent down to pick them up, and froze, the flowers were all dead, the leaves black and curled, the petals already pooling in the cellophane. Perhaps it was a mistake, maybe the flowers were meant to have been delivered earlier but been delayed somewhere. She looked for a delivery note, but there was none. That meant they had been hand delivered. She picked them up gingerly, buried within the dead stems was a note, it simply read "To Siobhan, our love is as dead as these blooms." Shaking slightly she looked around to see if anyone was watching, she whisked up the flowers and unlocked the front door as fast as possible, her fingers trembling as she tried to turn the key in the lock.

Once inside she called out to make sure no one was home, she wasn't expecting anyone to be there but she didn't want to be interrupted. There was no reply to her call. Holding the flowers as if they might explode in her hands she took them into the kitchen. Instinctively she went to put them in the sink, she almost smiled to herself at the futility of the act, then she laid the flowers on the kitchen table and unwrapped them. A dozen roses, she assumed they had once been red, but now they were decaying before her eyes. The note wasn't signed but Siobhan knew who had sent them.

Suddenly she felt sick, she rushed to the toilet but only a dry retching came out, she sank to the floor, letting her head rest against the cool porcelain. Her mind was filled with a hundred thoughts, what if one of the kids, or Dan had found them first, how did Niamh know where she lived, why was she so obsessed with her, what was going to happen now?

She tried to be practical, the first thing to do was to get rid of the evidence, make sure Dan didn't see the remnants of the bouquet. She put the cellophane in the main bin outside, then chopped the flowers up before throwing them into the garden waste bin. They lay on top of the bin, staring at her accusingly, Siobhan went back into the kitchen and found the food waste bin, she hurried back outside and threw that on top of the flowers in an effort to disguise them. They weren't as obvious now, she just had to hope that Dan didn't look too closely next time he put anything in the bin.

Once the flowers had gone she picked up her phone, she was about to text Niamh, but paused, was that actually a good idea or was this what Niamh wanted, to prolong the contact. She put the phone down and tried to marshal her thoughts. Tea, she needed tea.

Normally she didn't take sugar but she needed something to stop the shaking, and it was too early to open a bottle of wine, as sorely tempted as she was. The hot, sweet tea was exactly what she needed, and she felt her heart rate returning to nearly normal. *I need to think rationally, perhaps if I just speak to her, she'll understand how futile this is, and that she's risking her own relationship.*

Siobhan didn't know what made the thought come to her but she suddenly realised she had never met Gemma, she had always been away with family, or on course. Doubts began to form in her mind, was Niamh actually in a relationship with this Gemma or was this someone else that Niamh had pursued and fixated on. She began to rack her brains, trying to remember what Niamh had said about Gemma.

Where had they met? Law school, that's what she said, and she mentioned getting drunk coming back a Gray's Inn dinner. Gray's published a list of all barristers called every year, and the Law school they attended, she would just have to go through the lists and find a Gemma called the same year as Niamh, given fewer than a hundred people were called at any one time it should be a relatively short task.

Siobhan checked her watch, she had a couple of hours before school finished. She opened her laptop, she chose to enter private browsing mode, not entirely sure in her own mind who she was hiding her online activity from. She went to the Gray's home page and began to search through. First of all, she entered Niamh's full name, it popped up that she had been called by Gray's Trinity Term the year previously, perfect, that gave her a date to work with. Next she worked methodically through the names, Gemma Austin, she checked the Law school, Northumbria, nope, wrong one. There was only other Gemma listed, Gemma Harrington – Nottingham Law School. Bingo.

Siobhan wasn't quite sure what to do now she had the name, she remembered Niamh saying something about Gemma not being in pupillage, but she couldn't recall where she said she had been working. The obvious thing to do was to Google the name and see what came up.

She typed in the name, and hit enter. She noticed that her fingers had trembled slightly as she had typed – she tried to push the irrational fears away but she couldn't quite shake the feeling of fear and uncertainty.

Great, over two million hits, of which the first page was all Facebook links. This would get her nowhere. She paused before typing again, this time she wrote Gemma Harrington barrister. She knew that Gemma had not completed pupillage yet but thought it might narrow the field slightly.

Siobhan's mouth went dry as she read the first hit

"Aspiring barrister found dead in woods"

Her eyes began to swim in and out of focus. Following the link she read the article in full:

Gemma Harrington, 23, was found dead in Cannock Chase park this weekend. Police are not treating the death as suspicious. Local sources said Miss Harrington had recently finished law school and had hoped to become a Barrister however had not managed to obtain a placement so far. Her family declined to comment other than to say she would be greatly missed.

That's all it said. The obvious answer was suicide but Siobhan had a nagging doubt that it was as straightforward as that. She scrolled down through the next few hits.

The inquest into the death of Gemma Harrington, a young aspiring barrister who was found hanging in Cannock Chase, concluded today. The Coroner heard evidence from Miss Harrington's family who said that Gemma had been optimistic about obtaining employment.

The Coroner noted Miss Harrington had recently ended a relationship. Although no note was found the Coroner ruled that the death was suicide. Miss Harrington's family were too upset to comment as they left court.

Siobhan's blood ran cold, the line "recently ended a relationship" resonated and she couldn't get the phrase out of her head. So now she knew why she had never met Gemma. Where did that leave her though? Questions circled through her mind, why had Niamh lied to her, if Gemma was the one who ended the relationship why did she then kill herself? None of it made any sense and Siobhan sat staring at her laptop, unable to tear her eyes away from the search results. What should she do, what could she do? Was this why Niamh was being so possessive, because she had recently lost someone, or was it more sinister than that?

The criminal barrister in her took over, she needed to establish the evidence, find out the circumstances in which Gemma had died and whether there was more to it than had been reported in local papers. She also had to decide what to do about the flowers, confront Niamh or just ignore the incident in the hope that it was simply Niamh lashing out in anger.

Siobhan got up to make herself a fresh cup of tea, her legs felt wobbly beneath her as she carried the kettle over to the sink. Above all she had to prevent anyone else from finding out about the whole incident, she was acutely aware of not only the risk to her personal life but also her professional life too. She racked her brains. She sometimes prosecuted for Staffordshire CPS so knew a lot of the local lawyers, but if there hadn't been any prosecution considered then they wouldn't hold any paperwork. However, a dead body had been found, that of itself would have prompted an investigation, so the Police would have taken statements before the matter got to the Coroner, if she could speak to an officer she might get some information.

It was almost time for her to pick up Ben, ordinarily he went to after school club but as she was home early she wanted to make the most of her chance to see him. Closing the laptop she put her dirty mug in the sink then put her coat on to fetch Ben.

"What are you doing here Mom?"

"Nice to see you too Ben!"

"Sorry, just didn't think you were picking me up today"

"Well I finished early so thought we could maybe go to the shops and you can help me choose something nice for dinner"

"Cool, can we have pizza?"

"Let's see what they've got"

Ben chattered excitedly as they parked up in the local Sainsburys, Siobhan enjoyed these times, the meaningless chatter of a 9 year old with nothing more to worry about than which Lego set he wanted next. They picked out a pizza and some garlic bread then headed for home. Emily was back now too and seemed pleased to find her mother home at a reasonable time. Siobhan busied herself in the kitchen, trying to look relaxed so that nobody would be able to tell there was anything wrong. Every so often she glanced outside at the compost bin, thinking of the rotting flowers and all they represented.

She jumped when she heard Dan's key in the door. Get a grip, she told herself. She concentrated on keeping her face calm and neutral.

"Alright love, you're home early?"

"Yep, trial cracked so thought I'd come home and have some time with the kids" She felt the forced gaiety in her own voice and hoped that Dan wouldn't notice.

"How was your day?"

"OK, got most of the rewire done, got to go back tomorrow and finish it but shouldn't be a long one."

"Oh that's good"

"You ok? You look tired"

"Fine, just thinking about work, but I think I've got a day off tomorrow as I doubt I'll pick up another trial this week" She didn't feel fine, she felt sick and shivery but the last thing she wanted was for Dan to notice that, fortunately for her his mind was still on work and he didn't notice anything amiss.

Siobhan struggled to keep the conversation light throughout dinner, she was relieved when both of the kids disappeared to their rooms. Dan was slumped on the sofa, a reality show playing away in the background.

"I'm just going to read in bed for a bit"

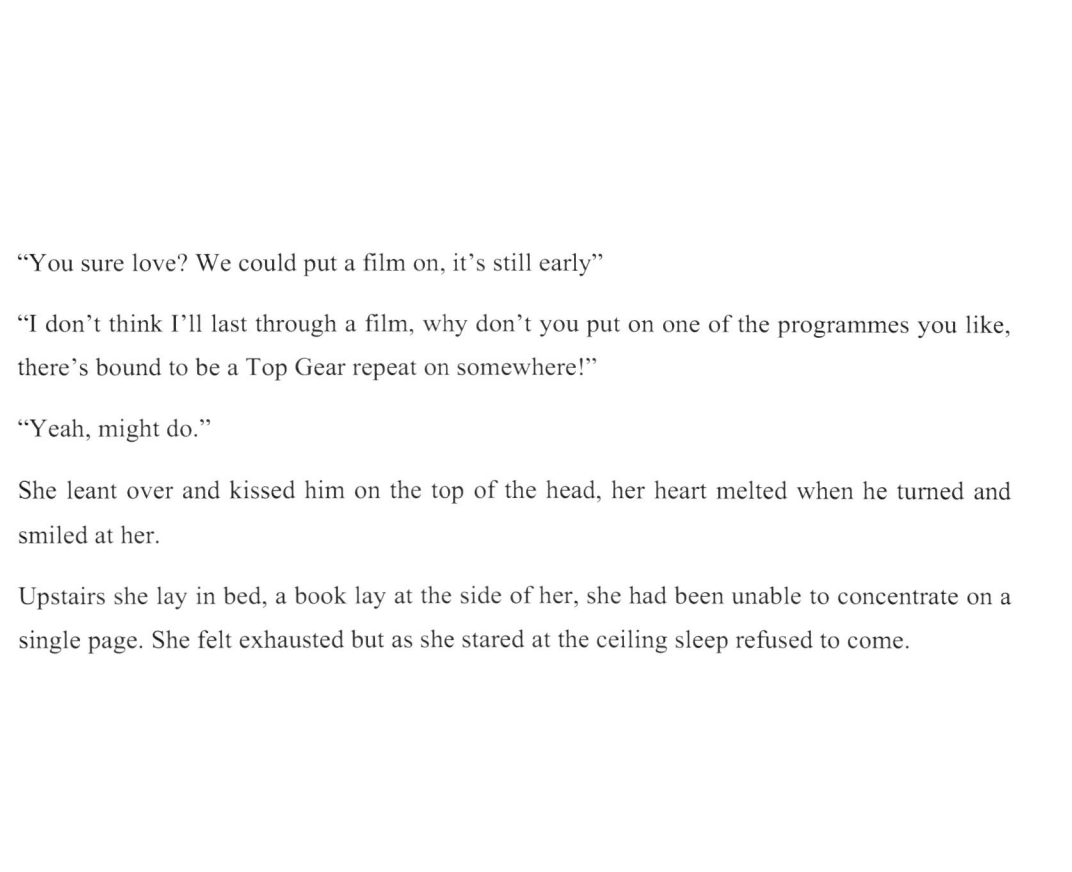

"You sure love? We could put a film on, it's still early"

"I don't think I'll last through a film, why don't you put on one of the programmes you like, there's bound to be a Top Gear repeat on somewhere!"

"Yeah, might do."

She leant over and kissed him on the top of the head, her heart melted when he turned and smiled at her.

Upstairs she lay in bed, a book lay at the side of her, she had been unable to concentrate on a single page. She felt exhausted but as she stared at the ceiling sleep refused to come.

Chapter eighteen

Siobhan slept fitfully, what little sleep she was had was punctured by vivid dreams in which Niamh was standing at the end of her bed, a knife in her hand. She awoke with a start and glanced at the clock, it was still before 6am. Realising she wouldn't be able to get back to sleep Siobhan crept out of bed. She pulled her dressing gown around her and tiptoed downstairs so as not to wake her sleeping family. She could feel the bags under her eyes, this was a tiredness unlike anything she had experienced before.

Overnight she had formulated an idea, she had been the prosecution junior on a murder trial in Stafford a few years previously, and had got on well with the Police team. She still had the contact details of a couple of the officers and she had decided to call them to ask about the Gemma Harrington case. What she hadn't decided yet was how to broach it with them, she didn't want to raise their suspicions but at the same time she wanted more information about what had happened.

Slowly the rest of the house came to life, Siobhan sorted out lunch boxes and PE kits before taking Ben to school. Once they had all gone she relished the silence. She sat for a while pondering her options before opening her phone and scrolling through her contacts.

The call was answered on the third ring

"DS Bright"

"Liz, hi, its Siobhan Flaherty, from the Ali case"

"Siobhan! Hello! Long time no hear, how are you?"

"Good thanks, busy, you know what it's like, mind you, if it weren't for the criminals we'd be out of a job so I can't complain. Anyway, to what do I owe the pleasure?"

"Obviously its lovely to speak to you, but I wondered if I could pick your brains, I've got a family friend who has just lost their teenage daughter, it looks like they committed suicide but the Police are involved. It's not something I've ever dealt with before and I wondered if it's something you've had any experience of so I could pass on a few tips, tell them what to expect?"

Siobhan held her breath, hoping that it sounded plausible.

"Oh your poor friend, that's awful. Yeah, suicide is obviously something we have to investigate, soon as a body gets found we are called in to make sure there's no foul play"

"So what sort of things do the Police do?"

"Well, the post mortem is pretty important, we want to confirm cause of death, make sure there are no signs of a struggle. We also search the area, see if anyone saw anything, other than the deceased. Obviously we're also checking for notes. Then we look into personal lives, have they got a motive for killing themselves, could someone else benefit, stuff like that"

"Sounds fairly comprehensive. I think I read about a suicide on your patch last year some time, similar to my friend, young girl hanged herself"

"Oh that was a sad case, pretty young kid, hanged herself in Cannock Chase"

"I think I read the Coroner ruled suicide, so did you have to investigate that one?"

"Yeah, that was one of ours, bit odd though, no note, usually when it's a youngster they want the world to know the pain they were in so you get a lengthy note, or nowadays a post on social media but there was nothing in that one"

Siobhan tried to keep her voice level "That is strange, was there anything else a bit odd about it?"

"Hmm, we had a witness who said he thought he heard an argument but that was a few hours before the body was found, plus he'd been drinking so no one took much notice. Poor girl also didn't do a great job of the knot, she had bruises all over the throat where she must have struggled and panicked as it tightened."

"That's awful. Makes you wonder what could drive someone so young to do something so drastic"

"Often it's not one big thing, it's a build-up of little problems that can seem insurmountable. This girl had been looking for a job, her parents said she'd just ended a relationship, although they had never met the bloke she was supposed to have been going out with"

"Did the Police speak to the bloke?"

"Didn't know who it was, as I say parents never met him, she didn't keep a diary, there was no note so we were never able to trace him"

"Assuming it was a him of course!"

"What do you mean?"

"Oh, just you know, in this day and age of political correctness we can't always assume it's a man, what with trans gender, non binary issues!"

The officer chuckled, "Yeah, bloody political correctness! Well we assumed it was a bloke, the Mom said flowers had been sent to the house and other gifts, sounded like a love sick young man to me! But they had no notes, or cards attached. Sad case, seemed a lovely young girl. Parents were devastated, they had no idea she was unhappy."

"So, can my friend expect family members to be interviewed?"

"Yeah, afraid so, it's fairly standard procedure, like I said, police are just trying to rule out anything criminal"

"Liz, you've been really helpful, thank you so much"

"My pleasure, please pass on my condolences to your friend"

"Thanks Liz, I will"

Siobhan felt guilty as she hung up the phone, but she justified the subterfuge to herself by considering what she had learned. A relationship where no one had met the other party, flowers sent to the house, no suicide note. Everything about Gemma's death made Siobhan more fearful about just what Niamh was capable of, either Niamh's obsession had driven Gemma to kill herself, or Niamh had actually been involved.

She felt sick, she couldn't speak to anyone about this without raising the alarm, but she was fairly sure she was now dealing with an obsessive woman who wouldn't take no for an answer.

She was shaken from her thoughts by the ringing of the doorbell. By the time she reached the door there was no one there but on the doorstep was a package. No address on it, no postage. Siobhan feared the worst. Gingerly she picked up the box and took it into her kitchen. She felt as if she were about to disarm a bomb as she pulled off the masking tape sealing the top. She reached inside, her heart pounding. A teddy bear, just a teddy bear. Siobhan laughed at her own cowardice, then turned the bear round, the eyes had been cut out, the stuffing was starting to fall out, there was hole in the chest where the heart would normally be, there too stuffing spilt out. Siobhan shrieked and threw the teddy down, it stared up at her as it lay on the floor, the stuffing eye holes glaring up accusingly.

Siobhan ran to the front door and flung it open, determined to find some trace of who had delivered it. She knew it was futile, the road was deserted, Niamh long gone.

She knew she had to do something, she just didn't know what. Was she in danger? Were her family in danger? Perhaps she ought to tell Dan, so he could protect himself? No, he wouldn't understand, their marriage would never recover. Perhaps she ought to just confront Niamh, call her out, let her know she wasn't going to be intimidated. She couldn't even begin to formulate the words. Perhaps she could warn Dan in another way, tell him to be vigilant but without revealing the real problem? If she told him about a defendant she had prosecuted perhaps, that way he wouldn't suspect but would still know to be on his guard. Yes, that was it, that's what she could do in the short term, and that would give her more time to figure out how to deal with Niamh in the long run.

The teddy bear still lay on the floor, Siobhan didn't want to touch it but she knew she couldn't leave it there. The bile rose on her mouth again as she approached it, the stuffing holes causing her to start shaking again. She almost put rubber gloves on just to pick it up but she knew she was being ridiculous, the main thing was to ensure neither Dan nor the children found it. She fetched an old carrier bag from under the sink and stuffed the hideous bear inside it, the box she folded down flat and threw into the recycling but she couldn't risk just leaving the bear in the bin. She put her coat on and walked to the local shops, looking for a rubbish bin in which she could finally dispose of the hateful toy.

Once home she couldn't settle, she tried to do some work but the cursor sat blinking at her on an empty screen. She picked up a book but couldn't concentrate on the words, the television was full of standard daytime fare, talk shows, property makeovers – none of which she could concentrate on.

She got up to make yet another cup of tea, not that she was thirsty, it was just a way of filling the time. As she waited for the kettle to boil she heard her phone ping with the sound of an email.

"Dear Siobhan

Thank you for volunteering to teach at this year's Pupils Advocacy Course. Please find attached the programme and training materials, which includes the timetable. We look forward to seeing you on Saturday and thank you for your continued assistance with the Circuit Education Programme."

Damn it, she had completely forgotten about that. Siobhan volunteered every year, all Pupils on circuit had to partake in a mandatory advocacy course, run over two days at a local conference centre. It was usually good fun and the Circuit provided plenty of booze at the evening meal, it was an informal way for the new barristers to meet more senior practitioners and Siobhan had always felt strongly about helping out the youngsters coming through. This year though Niamh would be on the course. She couldn't cancel now, it wouldn't be fair on the organisers, at the same time she wasn't sure how she would deal with being with Niamh for two days. She picked her phone and typed out a quick email.

Dear Tony

Thanks for the material. Just a quick note, one of our pupils is on the course this year, Niamh O'Brien, I think it would be useful for her to be in a different group to me so that she gets exposure to other advocacy trainers. Hope that's ok?

Yours

Siobhan

She pressed send and hoped that her email would at least give her some time to figure out how to deal with the weekend. More pressing though was what she would tell Dan.

The hours seemed to drag as Siobhan waited for him to return home from work. In an effort to pass the time she set about cleaning the house, getting on top of the mound of ironing that never seemed to diminish, and then prepping the veg for dinner. Finally it was time for her to collect Ben and once he was home safely she felt herself relax a little. Emily came back less than an hour later, she immediately disappeared to her room but at least she was home.

Dan walked through the door at 5.45pm, he looked exhausted.

"Cup of tea love?"

"Yeah, please, long day pulling wires today"

He slumped on the sofa, Siobhan left him alone for a few minutes, building up the courage to tell him yet another lie.

"Dan, I don't want to worry you, I just need to talk to you"

Dan looked up, his eyes immediately clouded with concern.

"What? What's wrong, are you ok?"

"I'm sure it's nothing, but chambers called, I've had a threatening letter from someone, the clerks open all mail unless its addressed as personal so they saw it and thought they ought to tell me."

"What do you mean threatening? Who is it?"

"It wasn't signed, but it's obviously somebody I prosecuted at trial, I haven't seen the letter but they say things like "You'll get what you deserve bitch" and "See how you like what's coming". "

"Well have chambers called the Police, have you called the Police?"

"No, I'm sure it's just empty threats, but at the same time, I want you to be on the lookout, if you see any cars you don't recognise and think someone may be watching the house, or if we get any letters at home, just, you know, think twice"

"For fuck's sake Siobhan, how can you be so calm? Why haven't you gone to the Police straightaway?"

"Dan, it's just words, I'm sure it's just someone letting off steam, the police have got enough on their plate without worrying about some nutter sending anonymous letters. I'm just saying to maybe keep an eye out that's all"

"What about the kids, are they in danger?"

"I don't think so, no"

"You don't think so? Shouldn't you be a damn sight more sure before you just wave this off as some nutjob sending letters, these are our kids Siobhan!"

"Don't shout at me, I know it's our bloody kids. If I thought they were in danger I would do something more, but it's me they are angry at, not them. Just calm down will you!"

Siobhan could see Dan curling his fist, then unfurling as he actively tried to calm himself.

"I told you about this just to be on the safe side, Ok. This isn't going to stop us living our normal lives, if anything else happens then I'll go to the police – would that make you happy?"

"Happy isn't the word I'd use. Shiv, I love you and the kids to bits, I don't know what I'd do if anything happened"

"It won't Dan. I didn't mean to panic you, I'm sorry. Come on, finish your tea, dinner's nearly ready"

Dan stood up and bearhugged Siobhan, she was taken aback by the intensity of it, she felt tears come to her eyes as she realised she would never be able to tell him the truth about what had happened.

Over dinner she tried to casually bring up the advocacy weekend. She didn't know why she was panicking, it was something she did every year so Dan would have no reason to suspect there was anything wrong but still Siobhan fought to control the tremble in her voice as she mentioned it.

"It's the advocacy weekend this weekend, I forgot to mention it before"

"Oh, right, same place as always?"

"Yeah, down in Northampton. I'll be leaving about 8am on Saturday but I'll be home for Sunday dinner"

In her own mind Siobhan thought her voice sounded too perky, that Dan was bound to notice the element of falsity, thankfully he was oblivious and didn't even mention the weekend again.

Siobhan felt sick, worry, guilt, it was all too much for her. She had to talk to Niamh just to try and make this stop before anyone got hurt.

Chapter nineteen

Siobhan's alarm rang a 7am, it always felt earlier somehow when it went off at the weekend. She had packed the night before so all she needed was a quick shower and a bite to eat. The children were still fast asleep, Siobhan poked her head around their bedroom doors before saying goodbye to Dan. He was in bed but was just rousing himself.

"I'm off now love"

"Alright, have fun, see you tomorrow"

"I'll try." She paused "Love you"

Dan looked a little surprised before replying "Love you too, you daft sod. Drive safely"

Traffic was light at this time on a Saturday morning. Siobhan spent the journey trying to work out what she was going to say to Niamh, whether to confront her, or to not mention it and see if Niamh said anything. She simply didn't know how to deal with anything like this.

The heater in the car was making her feel lightheaded so she wound her window down to try and get some fresh air, her head was pounding and she felt a tight sensation behind her eyes, she just wanted the weekend to be over and then to try and gain some semblance of control of her life, which she felt was rapidly spiralling out of her grasp.

She pulled up at the hotel, normally the sight of the grand old Manor House made her pause and smile, a weekend of good food and wine, and a chance to catch up with colleagues, but today she felt none of that relief. She looked around the car park, trying to spot whether Niamh was there already, she felt foolish as she remembered that Niamh didn't drive. Or did she? She no longer knew where the truth ended and the lies began with that woman. Trying not to shudder she hauled her suitcase out of the boot and dragged it across the car park to reception.

"Good Morning Madam"

"Morning, Siobhan Flaherty, here for the Midland Circuit training weekend"

"Of course, please sign in here and I will get your lanyard. You have been here before, yes?"

"Just a few times" grinned Siobhan "Many others here yet?"

"Yes, they are taking coffee in the lounge area if you would care to join them, your room is not yet ready but you are of course welcome to leave your suitcase here"

Siobhan took her lanyard and crossed the courtyard to the lounge, the hotel always provided snacks with the hot drinks and Siobhan usually put on at least a couple of pounds over the course of a weekend.

"Shiv, hi!"

"Tony, good to see you"

They air kissed before Tony began to busily introduce her to a number of the pupils

"We've got about 20 or so this year, not a bad turnout, not many doing crime which is always a shame but they're all bright as buttons."

"Great stuff, who I am teaching with?"

"Barry Jenkins, you know he never says no to a weekend of free booze!"

Siobhan liked Barry, he was a Senior Circuit Judge but still dedicated to circuit, he had a puppy like enthusiasm for these training weekends and the pupils were always in awe of being taught by a proper Judge. She glanced around nervously whilst making small talk with Tony, she still couldn't see Niamh and she hoped against hope that maybe she had decided not to come.

She spotted other colleagues and was delighted to see Sarah, she hadn't realised she was also teaching this weekend.

"Sarah!" Siobhan practically ran to her friend, grabbing her in a bear hug.

"Shiv! Darling! How have you been? I haven't seen you since the funeral, how are you bearing up?"

Siobhan felt a lump rise in her throat, it still felt raw to even think about her mother, but she also felt guilty, the problems with Niamh had been so overwhelming these last few weeks that she had pushed thoughts of her mother to one side, Sarah's question had brought them swiftly, and vividly to the surface.

"Oh God, I'm so sorry, I didn't mean to upset you, I'm such an arse!"

"No, it's Ok. Honestly, I'm fine until someone asks me if I'm fine" Siobhan smiled weakly, hoping to reassure her friend.

"Oh Shiv, look, tonight, you, me, a bottle of red in the bar after dinner and we are putting the world to rights. I've barely seen you and I need to know what's been going on!"

Siobhan thought to herself that Sarah wouldn't believe it even if she told her but she said nothing other than "Sounds like a plan, I'll maybe catch you at lunch?"

"Fab, don't be too harsh on those kids and I'll get the booze in for later"

Sarah busied herself getting another coffee, Siobhan smiled, relieved to have a friendly face here if need be.

"Right chaps and chapesses, if I could get you all in the main conference room for 9.15 we can get cracking"

Tony's jovial voice boomed across the coffee lounge and there was a flurry of activity as pupils and trainers gathered paperwork and laptops.

Siobhan took a seat in the conference room, she positioned herself towards the back of the room where she could spot everyone who came through the door. Various colleagues shouted out greetings as they poured through the door, the pupils all looked apprehensive, intimidated by the familiarity with which the barristers and judges all greeted one another.

Just before 9.15am Siobhan spotted Niamh, she felt her heart rate increase as she walked into the room, despite Niamh's behaviour towards her over these past few days Siobhan couldn't help but be struck by her beauty, and the memory of their illicit kisses.

Niamh looked around the room as she entered and when she saw Siobhan her eyes narrowed, Siobhan almost cowered before checking herself, she forced herself to sit upright in her chair and not to break eye contact. Niamh held her gaze for what felt like an eternity before moving away, Siobhan had to fight to stop herself from being sick. She tried to concentrate on what Tony was saying but all she could think about was Niamh.

Thankfully the first two hours of the morning were taken up with teaching in small groups. Barry bounded into their break out room, full of enthusiasm.

"Morning gang! So, I hope you have all done the prep and are ready for a fun weekend of advocacy training!"

The pupils looked at him nervously

"I'm Barry, this is Siobhan, we are both experienced criminal practitioners and by the end of tomorrow you will all have the confidence to get out there and be let loose on unsuspecting members of the public!"

Siobhan sat back and let him take over as he went around the room getting all of the pupils to introduce themselves, they all looked so young, Siobhan had to remind herself she had been in the job for over twenty years now. She missed the excitement of those early years, when every case was an adventure, a chance to prove yourself, now all she felt was weariness and cynicism.

Barry was calling upon the first pupil to open the case, Siobhan focused herself and started to make notes to give feedback.

By 11am the group was tiring, it had been an intense session and everyone was ready for a break. Barry released them and they all hurried over to the coffee lounge, eager to chat with their fellow pupils about how the morning had gone.

Siobhan hung back, from the room they were in she could see the front entrance to the coffee lounge and she didn't want to be there before Niamh arrived. Niamh came into view, chatting to someone Siobhan didn't recognise, presumably another pupil. Siobhan waited until they had gone in before following at a distance. She still hadn't made her mind up as to what she was actually going to say to Niamh when she finally had the chance to speak to her.

The lounge was buzzing with conversation and Siobhan mingled with her colleagues, enjoying the chance to see them out of court. Dress was typical barrister casual with all of the male barristers in a variation of red trousers, tweed jackets and Oxford shirts. Siobhan smiled to herself, we really are like sheep, she thought, we all dress the same, even at the weekend.

She chatted to Mohammed who had been in her group that morning "You did pretty well there, I thought your opening was very strong"

Mohammed smiled shyly "Thank you, I was so nervous"

"Perfectly natural, nerves give you an edge in court, I was always told that the day you are no longer nervous is the day you should hang up your wig"

There was a pause in the conversation and Siobhan saw Niamh walk past, forcing herself to sound casual she called out "Niamh, have you got a moment?"

Niamh stared at her and for a horrible moment Siobhan thought she was going to blurt out their sordid little secret, instead she took a breath and replied "Yes, of course"

Siobhan guided her outside, it was freezing and their breath hung heavy in the air but she didn't want any eavesdroppers casually listening in on their conversation.

"Hi"

"Hello"

"We need to talk"

"I disagree, you made your position quite clear, whilst you are married we have no future"

"That's not exactly what I said, you know what the issue is, I am married and we cannot be together, but that's not what I want to talk to you about"

"I have nothing more to say to you"

Niamh turned to walk away, Siobhan went to grab her arm but Niamh pulled away.

"Don't touch me"

The venom in her voice startled Siobhan and she dropped her hand, other pupils were starting to file outside and were looking at them closely. Siobhan didn't dare say anything further now, that sick feeling was back in her stomach and she had fight the urge to throw up in the courtyard.

"Come on Shiv, let's get cracking with the next sesh" Barry's cheerful voice boomed across the courtyard and Siobhan reluctantly returned to the conference room. She had half a mind to leave the training session but knew that her absence would raise more questions. It was no use, she would have to just get through this and try and confront Niamh again later, she couldn't live her life like this, panicking every time the doorbell went, or a strange car went past.

The remainder of the morning dragged, the barristers playing the witnesses did their best to liven proceedings up, deploying comedy accents, and answering questions literally, making the poor pupils work for their answers. Siobhan tried to throw herself into the process and focused on the feedback that she was giving, it was always heart warming to see the pupils growing in confidence and ability after just a few short hours and she soon became absorbed in the task. As the minutes ticked closer to lunch that familiar know returned to her stomach. She tried not to look at her watch but couldn't help glancing at it, her throat felt tight and her hands were sweaty. Get a grip she thought to herself, you're a grown woman!

The final student finished their cross examination at 12.58pm, Siobhan whispered a silent prayer of thanks and tried to casually saunter out of the conference room. They had an hour and half for lunch which Siobhan figured could give her plenty of time to eat with the Pupils, and then find Niamh and have a proper conversation with her.

The lunch room was humming with the excited chatter of the pupils, all growing in confidence and buoyed by the morning's work. Siobhan wished she felt as happy and carefree as they all appeared to be. She glanced around but there was no sign of Niamh. Reluctantly she joined the queue. Her mood was improved when she saw the lunch on offer and she was soon enjoying the poached salmon and Jersey Royal potatoes.

She sat down with a two of the other trainers and a group of the Pupils who were swapping horror stories from their first six months in pupillage. Siobhan sat back, happy to let the chat wash over, laughing every so often at one of the war stories but all the time watching the dining room for signs of Niamh.

She realised she hadn't checked in, so to kill time as she waited for food she walked down to reception.

"Hi, just wondering whether my room is ready yet? Flaherty, Siobhan Flaherty"

"Yes, one moment please and I will check this for you" There was a pause as the receptionist's fingers flew over the keyboard. "Yes, all ready now, you are in the main house, room 242. Here is the key and I think you left your luggage here too"

Siobhan signed for the key card and then hoisted her suitcase up. She trundled her case across the cobbles and up the two flights of uneven stairs, the downside of the beautiful old manor house was that they hadn't installed lifts back in the 17th century, still it was worth it for the character and history of the building. Her room was in the original part of the house, the room full of beautiful pieces of mahogany furniture, and tapestried curtains. The view was of the rolling fields of the Northamptonshire countryside and Siobhan wished for a moment that she could just stay like this, away from everyone, the stress of the problems she had created, but she knew that she had to confront Niamh and so with regret she locked up her room and walked with a heavy heart back to the dining room.

Siobhan spotted Niamh as she joined the queue for food, naturally she had opted for the salad bar. Niamh appeared alone, aloof from her fellow pupils. She selected just a few salad items and moved to a table a couple of meters away from Siobhan. Although there were others on her table Niamh said little, pecking at her food like a dainty bird. Siobhan tried not to stare, but she wanted to speak to Niamh before she disappeared from the dining room. She waited until Niamh had cleared her plate, then, pushing her chair back she confidently walked over to Niamh's seat.

"Niamh, hi, I've got that document you asked for, shall we go through it now?"

Niamh's eyes filled with confusion as the other pupils looked at her expectantly, before it dawned upon her what Siobhan was doing.

"Ok, give me a minute to finish up here"

Siobhan could feel the hate coming from Niamh's eyes but she sought to keep a bland smile on her face as the other pupils tried to work out what was going on. Time seemed to stretch as Niamh made a great play of straightening her cutlery and draining the last dregs of water from her glass, Siobhan shifted nervously from foot to foot and pretended this was all completely normal. Finally Niamh stood up and Siobhan ushered her away.

"The document is in my room" she said it loud enough for listening ears to hear, and watched as Niamh reluctantly followed her out of the dining room.

They walked up the carpeted stairs, their footsteps muffled by the heavy pile. Neither of them spoke and the silence weighed heavy in the air. Siobhan was full of trepidation as the door unlocked and they stepped into the empty room.

"Niamh, I know you sent the flowers, and the teddy"

Niamh stared at her with blank eyes. Siobhan felt her mouth go dry, she hadn't actually planned what she was going to say and now, standing alone in this room with Niamh she felt incredibly vulnerable.

"You shouldn't have sent them, you scared me"

Still no response. "What if one of my children had seen them?"

Siobhan had hoped to appeal to Niamh's humanity but the steel in Niamh's eyes made Siobhan shudder. She clearly wasn't getting through to her, it was if she was a robot.

"Tell me about Gemma"

"What about Gemma?" The reply was fired back and Siobhan jumped at the intensity of her response.

"You tell me, aren't you worried about her finding out about us?"

"That won't happen"

"Why won't it happen Niamh?"

"Just let me worry about that OK"

"It's because she's dead isn't she"

Her words had the same effect as if she had slapped Niamh, her face visibly recoiled and Siobhan saw fear in her eyes.

"I read the reports, she was found hanged in Cannock Chase last year. Why did you lie to me Niamh?"

"How dare you pry into my business! You had no right!"

"You lied to me" You created this fantasy life where you lived with her in a flat, and she was working and you were planning a future together, what the fuck was it all about?!"

Siobhan felt her anger bubble to the surface, she had suppressed it so much in the last few days but now she couldn't stop the words from tumbling out. "All that crap about meeting at Bar school, and her trying to get pupillage, you've made a fool of me!"

"It wasn't crap, we did meet at Bar school!"

"So why lie about the rest, what is going on?"

"Why do you care?"

"Because whatever happened has clearly affected you and the way you are behaving is frightening me!"

"Siobhan I love you, and I just want you, is that too much to ask?"

"Yes! I am married, I have kids, I'm sorry, but you knew that. What we had was fun, and don't get me wrong, it provoked feelings in me I never knew existed but I thought it was an affair for you too, you said you were in a relationship with Gemma, and now I discover she is dead, and I don't know what the fuck is going on anymore!"

Niamh began to sob, great, gasping sucks of air as the tears flowed from her face, Siobhan didn't know where to look or what to say, the anger began to give way to discomfort and she shifted nervously from foot to foot. Tentatively she put her arm around Niamh's shoulder, feeling her narrow blades as they shuddered up and down. Before Siobhan could stop her Niamh brought her face to Siobhan's and began to kiss her. Shocked, Siobhan tried to pull away

"No, Niamh, stop!"

Niamh looked at her blankly, the tears still fresh in her eyes. "Isn't this why you invited me into your room, this what you want"

"No, it's not, what the hell? I asked you here because I don't understand what you are playing at, you've been lying to me, acting like a fucking psycho and I want some answers!"

The silence stretched for what felt like an eternity, Siobhan felt the oppressive heat of the room, there was a buzzing in her ears and for a moment she thought she might actually pass out. Struggling to control her voice she took a deep breath,

"Niamh, why are you sending me dead flowers and teddies with their eyes taken out? Don't you understand that you are scaring me."

"You need to know how I feel, you can't just walk away from me, from this!"

"Jesus, Niamh! Is this why Gemma killed herself, because she couldn't cope with your obsession?"

There was a flash in Niamh's eyes and Siobhan felt genuinely afraid, had she come close to the truth about Gemma, too close? Was it worse than she thought?

"You wouldn't understand mine and Gemma's love, we were meant to be together, she just couldn't see that!"

"So what, what happened?"

"I'm not answering your questions, I don't owe you anything"

"You at least owe me an explanation as to why you lied about Gemma still being alive!"

"Because I miss her, and I can't accept that she's gone!" Niamh began to sob again, Siobhan stood looking at her uncomfortably, her hands dangled uselessly at her side. She didn't dare put her hands on Niamh again in case it was misconstrued.

"Gemma was depressed about work, she saw me getting on with my career, my life, and she couldn't handle it. All her life she had been a success and she just wasn't used to rejection. I tried to tell her that this was normal, that not everyone gets pupillage straight away but she just didn't want to listen. She began to drink and then night we had a huge argument and she took off. Police found her body a few days later, she'd killed herself."

"I read the Coroner's report, there was no mention of a suicide note or anything"

"I guess she didn't leave one"

"Did you give evidence at the inquest?"

"No, she hadn't come out to her family and I didn't want to cause them any unnecessary distress so I didn't get involved."

"But didn't you want them to understand why Gemma had killed herself?"

"At the time I wasn't thinking straight, I was so wrapped up in my own grief that I didn't even think about them"

Siobhan felt uneasy when she saw that Niamh appeared to have stopped crying so quickly, the emotion had gone from her voice, replaced by the cold, robotic tones that she had heard before when she had tried to end things with Niamh.

"So why did you send me those flowers, and that teddy?" Siobhan was trying to keep her voice even, and not let the anger seep through.

"I couldn't face the idea of losing you as well, not so soon after losing Gemma. I didn't mean to scare you, I just needed you to know what you meant to me"

"Ok, but it has to stop now, I've explained why"

"I know, I'm sorry, please understand what I was going through"

Siobhan still felt uneasy but she couldn't face any more tears or shouting. "Come on, let's go back to the training, then tonight just enjoy the meal, maybe even have a glass or two of red together?"

Niamh smiled weakly at her and Siobhan finally relaxed slightly, maybe this would be ok, no one would find out and she could put all of this madness behind her.

Siobhan opened the door and ushered Niamh back towards the training session, she pulled her door closed behind her and then joined Niamh at the top of the stairs.

The landing was quiet, everyone was still enjoying the break before the madness began again.

The last thing Siobhan was aware of was a heavy shove in the small of her back, and then windmilling in space as she fell through the air, towards the heavy flagstone floor at the bottom of the stairs.

Chapter twenty

"Miss, miss, are you OK?"

Siobhan felt as if her body was floating, she could feel the cold surface of something pressing against her cheek but struggled to work out what it was. She began to open her eyes but a painful flash tore through her skull and she thought she was going to be sick.

"Shall I call an ambulance?"

She was aware of voices talking over her, and the presence of feet near her. A gentle hand reached out and shook her shoulder. Siobhan groaned.

"Don't move, you might have broken something"

Siobhan tried to speak but her mouth seemed full of cotton wool, she realised the chill she could feel was the flagstones underneath her. She coughed and immediately another wave of nausea passed over her, this time the urge was too strong and she felt herself being sick before a wave of grey passed over her and slumped back into unconsciousness.

As she slowly came around she could hear a chatter of voices, and she was aware that a blanket had been placed over her. For one sickening moment she contemplated that she had actually died and these people were talking over her corpse, then she realised she could smell the vomit in her own hair, and she reached her hand to push it away, wincing at the sudden movement.

"Woah, take it easy, you've had a bad fall"

One of the hotel employees was crouching next to her, trying to offer words of reassurance, but Siobhan could feel her heart hammering with fear. Slowly, she pushed herself up, noting with relief that her arm didn't seem to be broken.

"I'm Ok" she croaked, realising how wrong that was as her vision blurred. She tried to focus and saw the concerned faces of the hotel staff surrounding her. "Did any of you see what happened?"

"No Miss, I was just clearing the grand hall for tonight and when I came out I found you at the bottom of the stairs, you must have taken a hell of a bang"

Siobhan looked around trying to see if anyone from the course was there, all she could see was a blur of uniforms.

"I have to go, I have to…"

"You're not going anywhere, you've got to be checked out" The voice cut across her, Siobhan didn't have the strength to try and argue.

"Do you think anything is broken?" She had already managed to pull herself up into a sitting position, and although it was painful she was able to turn her neck and head. She looked down at her legs and saw that they were twisted, she knew she had to try and move them, if Niamh was capable of this then who knows what she might do next. Fear ran through her as she realised Niamh knew where she lived.

"Seriously, don't try and move, you could do more damage"

Siobhan waved a hand at the person speaking "I have to get up, I have to go." She tried to move to pull herself up, but collapsed in a cry of pain as what felt like a rod of fire tore through her leg. Hot tears pricked her eyes, she was consumed with feelings of rage and frustration.

One of the bar staff came running over with a First Aid kit "Shall I get someone from the course over here?"

"Erm, yeah, my friend Sarah, Sarah Downing, she's teaching one of the groups, I'm not sure which room she's in though"

"Don't worry, we'll find her, just try not to move"

The Barman with the First Aid kit gingerly lifted Siobhan's ankle, Siobhan winced in pain.

"Sorry love, just trying to see if its broken. I think you might be lucky and have just sprained it"

"Oh great, yeah I feel really lucky!" Siobhan looked up and saw the Barman's embarrassed face, "Sorry, didn't mean to sound sarcastic, thanks for helping, it's just really bloody painful"

"Do you want to see if you can straighten it?"

"Yeah, can you give me a hand?"

Siobhan pulled herself up slightly straighter and gently prodded her ankle, slowly she began to unfurl her legs, the Barman held out his hand in support. The pain nearly made her pass out again but she was finally able to straighten both legs, neither was bleeding but her left foot was beginning to swell alarmingly and it felt tight within her jeans.

"I really think we should call an ambulance"

"No, it's OK. I'll get my friend to drive me to a hospital, I don't think its broken, I don't want to waste Paramedics time if I can get there myself"

The staff looked doubtful but any reply was cut off by the arrival of Sarah

"Shiv, what the fuck happened!"

"I fell, I'm ok, just sore, and a bit embarrassed"

The lie tripped easily off her tongue, Siobhan didn't have the time or energy to even begin to explain what had happened, right now all she wanted was to be off the flagstone floor and hunting down the bitch that had put her here.

"Can you stand?"

"I think so, can someone help me?"

A chair appeared from the dining hall and two pairs of strong hands held her as she tried to get to her feet. She couldn't bear any weight on her left foot and the swelling seemed to be getting worse, she sat down on the chair with a heavy thud.

"I'll get you some water"

"Thanks, Sarah, I'm sorry to be a pain, but do you think you'd be able to drive me to hospital? I don't want to be stuck at one out here, I was hoping to get to Good Hope, least that way I'm near my family if I have to stay in"

"Yeah, sure. Give me a few minutes just to go and tell Tony and my group what's happening. I'll come back as soon as we're ready to go."

"Great, I don't suppose someone could get my things from my room could they?"

One of the hotel employees took Siobhan's key card and hurried away, another brought some water as well as a welcome mug of hot, sweet tea. Siobhan drank it gratefully, noticing that her hand trembled slightly as she took the mug.

Her suitcase was returned to her just as Sarah arrived back with her car keys. Two of the staff helped her to her feet and gingerly Siobhan limped to the car park, the nausea passed over her again and it took all of her resolve not to collapse into the staff's arms. She didn't want them to know how badly injured she was lest they try and persuade her to go in an ambulance, her focus was on getting home and keeping her family safe. She was trying to work out how long she had been unconscious for and how much of a head start Niamh had.

Sarah opened the passenger door of her car and ushered Siobhan in before putting her suitcase in the boot.

"What are you going to do about your car?"

"I'll worry about that later, Dan can hopefully drive a friend down tomorrow and pick it up"

Sarah looked worried but said nothing as they pulled out of the car park. The country road leading away from the hotel was quiet and Sarah enjoyed the chance to put her foot down.

"Good Hope is the hospital in Sutton isn't it?"

"Yeah, but I don't want to go there?"

"Do you want to go somewhere more local"

"Sarah, I'll try and explain in a minute but I need to make a phone call, just head towards the M6 for now"

Sarah looked across, puzzled, Siobhan didn't notice as she was busy rooting in her handbag, trying to locate her mobile phone which had naturally sunk to the bottom and was doing its best to evade her. Retrieving it with a sigh of relief she hit the speed dial and waited anxiously for Dan to pick up.

The phone rang out, Siobhan racked her brains trying to remember if Dan had said he was going out anywhere, or whether the kids had another party or play date. She willed Dan to pick the phone up, but it simply rang out. Frustrated, she hung up, then immediately dialled Dan's mobile. It rang, and rang. The fear grew in Siobhan's stomach.

"Dan, when you get this message can you call me, please, its urgent. Also, make sure the doors are locked at home, and don't let the kids out. I don't mean to panic you, but please call me. Love you"

Sarah was trying valiantly to concentrate on the road whilst also trying to work out just what the hell was going on.

"Siobhan, where are we going and what on earth has happened?"

Siobhan took a deep breath, she wasn't ready to explain herself, she had kidded herself that no one would ever find out about her indiscretion, but now she had no choice.

"Oh God, I don't even know where to start. I don't want to go to hospital, I need to get home to check on my family because I'm worried that something might have happened to them"

"What?! Why haven't you called the Police, what the fuck is going on?"

"If I call the Police then this all comes out, I'm only telling you now because I've got no choice"

Sarah waited, impatiently, anxious to know what was happening but not wanting to interrupt her friend.

"OK, so, basically I've had an affair"

"Fuck off!"

"Oh, it gets worse. Erm, so, you know our pupil, Niamh"

"Yeah"

"Well, her."

Sarah sat in stunned silence, Siobhan felt her cheeks going red, just saying it aloud made her feel like an embarrassed schoolgirl admitting to her first crush.

"So, you're what, gay?"

"Erm, no, I don't think so, I mean I still love Dan, but perhaps, maybe there is another side to me that I, er, maybe didn't know about, or, er acknowledge" Siobhan was struggling to put into words just exactly what she had been going through these last few months, she didn't want to put a label on it, she wasn't sure she could, but she felt her friend couldn't understand that it wasn't as simple as being gay, straight, or bisexual, or whatever the hell she now was.

"So, is she going to tell Dan or something, is that what's going on here?"

"I think it could be more serious. I tried to break it off with her, I knew how stupid I'd been, but she got really needy, like massively creepy. She also told me that she was in a relationship, but it turns out her previous girlfriend died and I don't know if she killed herself or something else"

"Something else?"

"There are some question marks around the death that just creep me out. Anyway, this afternoon I tried to talk to her about it, and I thought I'd got through to her. We both left my room to go back to the conference room, then when I was standing at the top of the stairs, she pushed me. I think she was trying to kill me, but also trying to make it look like an accident. Now I don't know what she's capable of, and I think Dan might be in danger"

"Why the fuck haven't you called the Police?!"

"Because. Because the moment I do this all comes out, it's one thing telling you, but if the Police get involved then there's no way Dan isn't finding out, plus she's a pupil for fucks sake. I'm a tenant, I'm pretty sure I've breached several rules of the Code of Conduct, so not only does everyone in chambers find out, but there's a strong chance that the Bar Standards Board decide to take away my practising certificate too."

Sarah exhaled "Oh Shiv, what a mess!"

"That's a fucking understatement"

Siobhan sat morosely looking at the passing cars, she'd messed everything up, there was no way Dan wasn't going to find out about this. What if Niamh really was trying to kill him, or the kids, just the thought of it nearly made her sick with fear.

"So, what are you going to do?"

"Dunno. I just know I can't go to hospital. I figured if at least I get home I can make sure Dan and the kids are safe, then if she tries anything I can maybe stop her, talk some sense into her, but at least I'll be there, rather than stuck in the middle of the bloody countryside"

"And what exactly are you going to do when you can't even walk?"

"Sarah I can't call the Police, I'm not ready for all of this to come out, and if I get home to Dan before she gets there then maybe I can convince him she's crazy and he won't believe what she says. Perhaps she won't try and do anything to them, I'm the one she's pissed off at"

"That's your grand plan, hope for the best?"

"Well what do you suggest?"

"Give me a minute. Come on, we're intelligent women, there's got to be a way to sort this without anyone else getting hurt."

Siobhan found the silence in the car suffocating. She picked her phone up and tried Dan's mobile again. Still no answer. "Dan, its Siobhan, please, please call me when you get this"

She tried to calculate how much of a head start Niamh had on her, she could only have been unconscious for a few minutes but all of the toing and froing about going to hospital had delayed her, she reckoned by the time she left the hotel Niamh had been gone at least 25 minutes. Surely Niamh couldn't have reached Sutton already?

"Can you put the sat nav on?"

"I know where you live Shiv"

"I know, I just want to see what it says about traffic and how long it will take us to get there"

"Ok," Sarah pressed a few buttons

"You will reach your destination in 42 minutes"

"42 minutes, so if she's got half hour head start she still shouldn't be there. Any chance you can put your foot down?"

"You don't seriously think she would actually hurt Dan and the kids do you?"

Siobhan didn't answer.

"Oh God, you really do. I'll get there as soon as I can, OK. I've been thinking, Why don't you call Dan again, but this time tell him about Niamh, not that you two have had an affair, but that she's had a breakdown and is delusional. That way if she does get to him first, maybe he won't believe anything she says, and will just think she's a crazy person."

"Do you think that'll work?"

"You got any better ideas?"

Siobhan didn't answer, instead she picked up her phone for a third time. It rang, Siobhan thought it was going to answer phone, but at the last moment Dan picked up.

"Shiv, I've just got your messages. Are you OK?"

"Dan, oh thank God, no, I'm not ok. Where are you?"

"Just pulled up at home, the kids and I have been at the cinema and I forgot to turn my phone on after the film. What's going on?"

"Look, I'm coming home, I don't want you to worry, but there's this girl from work, Niamh. She was on the advocacy course and, well it didn't go so well, I think she's got some issues cos she's kind of flipped out and is ranting about hurting people"

"What's that got to do with me?"

"I just think she might come to our house?"

"Why the hell would she do that?"

Sarah mouthed at Siobhan "You were her teacher, she took it personally"

Siobhan didn't follow for a moment, then realised what Sarah was saying, she relayed it to Dan "It's because I was the one teaching her, and I think she took it really personally, so I think she might go to our house"

"That makes no sense, its just advocacy, why would she freak out like that?"

"I think she's got mental health issues, and, er, she's focused on me cos I was the one critiquing her at the time, and I think she's just had a melt down"

Siobhan could hear the confusion in Dan's mind as he tried to process what she was saying.

"Dan, are you in the house yet?"

"Yeah, I'm just in the hall now"

"Are the kids inside?"

"Yep, safe and sound"

"Listen, I'll be home in less than half an hour, lock the door, keep an eye out for any strange cars and just, well, be careful ok"

"OK, I still don't really get what's happening. Should I call the Police?"

"No, she hasn't actually done anything yet, and I don't want to, er, jeopardise her career by getting the police involved unnecessarily, so just sit tight, and I'll be there soon." She paused "Love you, Dan"

"Love you too, you daft apeth, I'll see you soon"

Siobhan was trembling as she hung up the phone. "Do you think he bought it?"

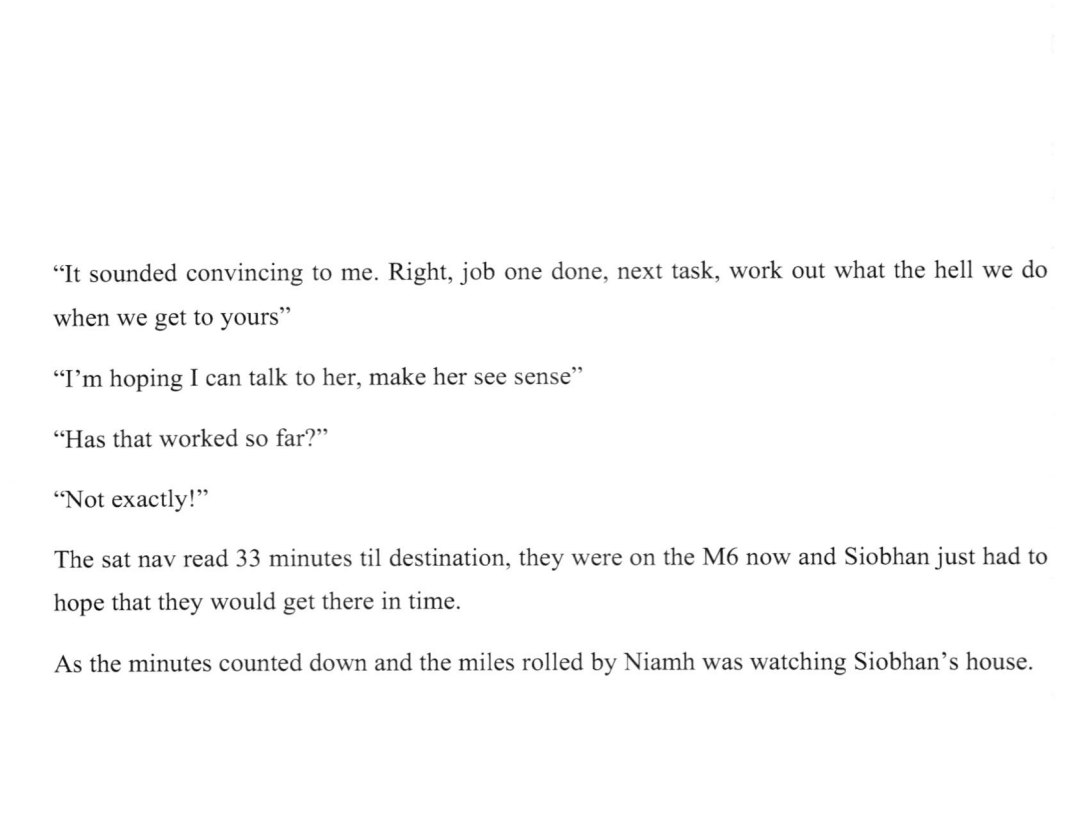

"It sounded convincing to me. Right, job one done, next task, work out what the hell we do when we get to yours"

"I'm hoping I can talk to her, make her see sense"

"Has that worked so far?"

"Not exactly!"

The sat nav read 33 minutes til destination, they were on the M6 now and Siobhan just had to hope that they would get there in time.

As the minutes counted down and the miles rolled by Niamh was watching Siobhan's house.

Chapter twenty one

Dan looked uneasily out of the bedroom window, he couldn't spot any cars he didn't recognise. The road was quiet, surely he would see someone if they approached the house. He had told the children to play in their rooms and then gone round the house, checking all of the doors and windows. Part of him didn't quite believe that someone would actually come to his house just because of an argument about advocacy teaching, but the stress in Siobhan's voice was real and that was enough for Dan to take this seriously.

Siobhan was now just five minutes away from home, she still hadn't considered what she was actually going to do if Niamh was there.

"Sarah have you got anything in the car that I could use as a weapon?"

"A weapon? Jesus! Siobhan if you are thinking about weapons then you should call the bloody Police!"

"I've told you, I can't, everything is at stake here Sarah, don't you get that?"

"I do, and I am your friend, and I want to help, but I've got a family of my own, I don't want to get involved in something that sees me getting hurt!"

"I'm not asking you to get hurt. Can you drop me at the corner of my road, then you can go"

"Right, and how exactly do you propose to tackle her if she's there, you can barely walk, look at your ankle, even I can see its swelling up!"

"I don't want you to get hurt"

"I don't want to get hurt, I'm a wimp. I want you to see sense and call someone who can actually do something about this!"

"Alright, look, drop me at the house, you stay outside. I've got my phone on me, if I need help then I promise I will call the Police, or try and signal for you to call the Police. How does that sound?"

"Makes more sense than you trying to deal with this by yourself."

Siobhan could see her home, she looked around but could there was no sign of disturbance, perhaps Niamh had come to her senses after all.

Sarah pulled up on the drive and turned the engine off. Siobhan opened her door, and winced as she put her foot on the ground, she had to hold on to the car door to steady herself, after a moment's pause she was stable and began to limp the few feet towards her home. She glanced nervously over her shoulder, Sarah gave her a reassuring thumbs up through her open window. Her hand shook slightly as she tried to put the key in the lock, taking a deep breath she calmed herself down and managed to open the front door.

"Dan, its me, are you OK?"

"All fine, I'm in the lounge"

Siobhan exhaled and called out to Sarah "Its OK, she's not here. I'll be OK now"

"Do you want your stuff?"

"Yeah, could you pass it over and I'll get Dan to help carry it in"

Sarah opened her car door and went to her boot, shaking her head in disbelief that this was actually happening. In the meantime Siobhan called for Dan to come and pick up the bags.

"I've just nipped to the loo" replied a distant voice.

Siobhan rolled her eyes. She hugged Sarah as she dropped the luggage on the floor. "Look, I'm really sorry you got pulled into all this. Thanks so much for giving me a lift home, can I trust that this won't go any further?"

"My lips are sealed. But you need to sort this out before anyone else gets hurt. Call me if you need me"

"Will do. Promise"

Sarah hugged her friend and returned to the car, she waited to see if Dan would appear to help with the case but when he hadn't after a few minutes she shrugged her shoulders and pulled off the drive. Siobhan watched her go, and waved gratefully, silently cursing Dan for choosing right then to decide he needed the loo so desperately.

Siobhan closed the door behind her, and pulled the chain across, some of the tension she had felt on the journey back began to dissipate, she was relieved that whatever had happened at the hotel seemed to have lanced the boil of Niamh's anger. She struggled to lift the suitcase further into the hall, giving up as it fell against the bottom step of her stairs.

She limped slowly towards the lounge, then froze with shock as she opened the door.

Dan was standing in the centre of the room, Niamh holding his arm with a knife pressed against his throat.

The world swam before her but before she could respond Niamh spoke "Do not say or do anything, if you do, I will kill him. Are we clear?"

The threat sounded even more sinister in Niamh's native accent, an accent Siobhan had thought so charming only a matter of months previously.

"Sit down on the sofa. Now"

Siobhan looked pleadingly at Dan, whom she noticed was actually crying. She tried to think about the last time she had seen him cry, her mind flashed back to Emily's birth when her big, strong man had melted as he held his first born child in his arms. He had sworn that day to always protect her and now here he was, standing in the lounge of his own house, a crazed woman with a knife to his throat, holding him hostage.

"I said sit!"

Siobhan reacted and sank to the sofa. "Where are my children?"

"Upstairs, safe, for now. What happens next depends very much on whether you are sensible and do as I say"

Siobhan nodded, dumbly. Dan was still in the middle of the room, she noticed a pin prick of blood had appeared at the point where the knife met his throat.

"Now, Siobhan, aren't you going to introduce me properly to your husband?"

Siobhan tried to speak but her tongue had turned to sandpaper.

"Come on Siobhan, use those words you're so famed for!"

"Dan, this is Niamh O'Brien"

"And who am I?"

Siobhan hesitated, she wasn't ready for this, but she knew she had no choice.

"Who am I Siobhan?" The dark menacing tone was there again.

"What do you want me to say Niamh?" Siobhan started at her, hopelessly.

"I want you to tell your husband the fucking truth!"

Niamh almost spat the words out, Siobhan could see the confusion in Dan's eyes as he tried to work just what exactly was happening in his own lounge.

"Please Niamh, it doesn't need to be like this!"

"Siobhan, either you tell him, or I do and I slit his fucking throat, then your children's, and finally I will make sure I stab you in such a way that when the Police get here, they think good old Siobhan has finally lost it and killed her family before turning the knife on herself. And if you don't think I am capable of that then you really don't know me at all."

"I don't know you, Niamh! I don't understand where this rage has come from, why would you want to hurt my innocent children?" Her voice began to break and she knew she was verging on the edge of hysteria.

"You weren't thinking of the children when you were fucking me, were you Siobhan?!"

Dan's eyes grew wide as he looked first to his wife, then to Niamh, dawning realisation coming over him. "No, Siobhan, she's lying, surely?"

Siobhan couldn't answer, sobs began to emanate, a deep, howling animal cry of pain.

"Mom?" She could hear Emily's concerned voice calling from upstairs. Niamh looked at her questioningly "Your choice Siobhan"

Using every ounce of resolve Siobhan possessed she called out to her daughter "It's Ok, Emily, I'll be up in a bit, just stay in your room for a minute"

"That's better, now, what would you like to tell your husband?"

"How did you even get in here?"

"Oh you're so fucking suburban! Who actually has one of the fake stones with a spare key at their back door. Do you think I'm stupid Siobhan? Now, tell Dan the truth!"

Siobhan looked at Dan, the pain behind his eyes so obvious, she was overwhelmed with the guilt of what she had done. "I'm so sorry Dan." Her voice was barely a whisper.

Niamh's face was breaking into a sly smile. "Don't you want to know the details, Dan?"

Dan shook his head, but Niamh continued "Your wife clearly wasn't getting what she needed from you, so she came to me. You should have felt her, Dan, she was wet for me"

Siobhan tried to stifle a sob, Dan couldn't look her in the eye.

"Niamh, please, what do you want?"

"I want you Siobhan, and if I can't have you, then no one can!"

"Please, Niamh, stop. I'm sorry, ok, I'm so, so sorry!"

"Stop fucking apologising, you're lying again, you're only sorry for yourself!" Niamh was shouting now, her voice carried through the house and Siobhan knew it would only be a matter of time before either Emily or Ben came downstairs. Sure enough, she heard the tell tale creak of the staircase.

"Emily don't"

Too late, Emily had already walked into the lounge. Her eyes took in the scene before her, her mother, sobbing on the sofa, her father stood in the middle of the room with a woman holding a large kitchen knife to his throat.

"Mom!"

Niamh lunged towards Emily. Siobhan felt as if she watching a film unfold in slow motion, she saw the glint of the knife in Niamh's hand, and threw herself at her feet. She was no rugby player but the movement was sufficient to just knock Niamh off her stride, and her legs buckled slightly. Niamh began to fall to the floor, the knife flailing in her hand. As she fell her body twisted, trying to rid her of her assailant, who held on to her legs even as she herself lay on the floor. Siobhan felt the knife before she saw it, Niamh had managed to lash out and strike Siobhan's face. Hot blood began to run down her cheek.

Dan woke from the stupor that had engulfed him, his daughter was still dangerously close to Niamh, who was waving the knife in an attempt to slash at Siobhan. Dan jumped on Niamh, the force of the impact knocking the knife from her hand. It skidded along the floor, coming to rest feet away from Niamh's out stretched hand. Niamh shrieked in both fear and anger. Siobhan was the first to react, she rolled away from Niamh's kicking legs and crawled towards the knife. Straining with every tendon her fingertips Siobhan felt the handle of the knife just within her grasp. Her hands closed around the wooden grip, without thinking Siobhan pulled the knife towards her, then lashed out. The knife plunged first into Niamh's shoulder, Siobhan pulled it out, and struck again, this time the knife sliced Niamh's arm. Blood spurted out and Siobhan knew she had hit an artery.

The noise was overwhelming, Emily was screaming, Ben had appeared at the door, and had also begun to howl, Niamh was shouting and swearing, blood was covering the floor. Niamh tried to scramble to her feet but the strength was ebbing out of her body, and Siobhan still had the knife. Using the last of her resolve Siobhan once more stabbed out, the knife went deep into Niamh's chest, with only the hilt preventing it from running almost entirely through her. Niamh collapsed, staring in disbelief at the weapon protruding from her body.

The room was silent for a moment, before being punctuated by Emily's crying. Siobhan wiped her cheek, staring in disbelief at the blood that came away on her hand. Niamh lay still on the floor, blood pooling around her. Ben and Dan both stood wide eyed in disbelief, Siobhan noticed the fear had caused Ben to wet himself. Nobody said anything, all eyes fixated on the dead body in the middle of the floor.

Siobhan was the first to speak "Dan, I'm so sorry"

Dan looked at her with hurt and confusion. "How could you?" And then he began to cry.

Siobhan sank to the floor, in one respect it was over, but she knew this was only the beginning.

Chapter twenty two

NINE MONTHS LATER

Siobhan groaned as her 5.45am alarm rang out. Her arm felt for the button and then quickly drew back under the quilt. The flat was cold, she was trying to save money by not putting the heating on.

She dressed quickly, pulling on warm clothing, knowing the warehouse would be bitter on a day like today. Her fingers trembled as she tried to do up her boot laces, a combination of cold and the effects of the drink from the previous night wearing off.

She couldn't face eating, she boiled the kettle to make a flask of tea to bring with her. Tears rolled down her cheek as she waited for the drink to brew. Her mind turned to her children, only another three days before she could see them.

The repercussions of Niamh's death were still being felt. The Police had been called, she and Dan had both been arrested on suspicion of murder. It had taken two days of interviews, the testimony of her children, and Sarah, and then weeks of review, including forensic analysis of the blood spatter, before the Police confirmed that neither of them would face charges. As a result of Niamh's actions Police had reopened the case of Gemma Harrington and determined that her death was not in fact suicide, she had been strangled with a rope, before the body had been moved to the woods and made to look like a hanging.

Once the Police investigation was over the Bar Standards Board had commenced its own investigation, it found that Siobhan had breached the Code of Conduct by failing to act with honesty and integrity, in having an affair with a pupil Siobhan had abused her position of trust and thus diminished public confidence in her. She had been disbarred, thus bringing her 22 year career to a juddering halt.

Dan had left her, or rather, she had been forced to leave him. They had tried for a few weeks but every time he looked at her all he could see was betrayal and the danger Siobhan had placed their children in. He had stayed in the house, and the children had stayed with him. Siobhan had moved into a flat in Wylde Green, two bedrooms, so that the children could still stay over, but small enough that she could afford it on her new wage, no longer able to work in law anymore she had been at a loss, what happened with Niamh haunted her, she just wanted a job where she could turn up, not interact with anyone, and leave again. She had considered retraining but she struggled to concentrate on even the most minor tasks. Sarah had tried to encourage her to have counselling, but Siobhan felt a need to punish herself, by taking a menial job and working through her grief. As a picker at a warehouse she could simply go to work, do her shift and leave again, chatter on the floor was discouraged, which suited her perfectly.

It meant the every day stresses of the Bar had gone, replaced by worries about having enough money to heat the flat every month.

Dan was civil to her, but their relationship consisted of him dropping the children at her flat every other Friday evening. He would remain in the car as Siobhan stood forlornly at the communal entrance to her block of flats.

Friday nights when she didn't have the children involved Gogglebox on TV and a cheap bottle of wine as she drank herself into a stupor.

As she tightened the strap of her cycle helmet, ready for the 3 mile ride to work Siobhan wiped away her tear. This was her life now, alone, broke, her family and career stripped away from her.

She cycled up to the Birmingham Road, waiting for the oncoming bus. She was done, the strains of the last year were too much. As the headlights approached she rode as fast as she could into the road. The bus driver didn't even have time to hit the brakes. With a sickening crunch Siobhan found the oblivion she now sought.